D0924208

# BUSHWHACKERS
## — AT THE —
# CIRCLE
# Ⓚ

*Also by Chet Cunningham*
*in Large Print:*


Battle Cry
Fort Blood
Renegade Army
Sioux Showdown
Flagstaff Showdown
Line Rider's Revenge
Outlaws: Avengers
Outlaws: Dead Man's Hand
Outlaws: Ride Tall or Hang High
Outlaws: Rio Grande Revenge
Outlaws: Six Guns

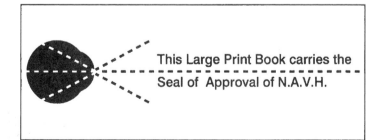

This Large Print Book carries the
Seal of Approval of N.A.V.H.

# BUSHWHACKERS
## – AT THE –
# CIRCLE

K

## CHET CUNNINGHAM

WHEELER
PUBLISHING

LP W        22 95
Cunningham, Chet.
Bushwhackers at the Circle K

Published in 2005 by arrangement with
Chet Cunningham.

Wheeler Large Print Western.

The text of this Large Print edition is unabridged.
Other aspects of the book may vary from the original edition.

Set in 16 pt. Plantin.

Printed in the United States on permanent paper.

**Library of Congress Cataloging-in-Publication Data**

Cunningham, Chet.
    Bushwhackers at the Circle K / by Chet Cunningham.
        p. cm. — (Wheeler Publishing large print westerns)
    ISBN 1-59722-074-4 (lg. print : sc : alk. paper)
    1. Ranchers — Fiction.  2. Large type books.  I. Title.
  II. Wheeler large print western series.
  PS3553.U468B87 2005
  813'.54—dc22                     2005016267

# BUSHWHACKERS
## — AT THE —
# CIRCLE
# Ⓚ

As the Founder/CEO of NAVH, the only national health agency solely devoted to those who, although not totally blind, have an eye disease which could lead to serious visual impairment, I am pleased to recognize Thorndike Press★ as one of the leading publishers in the large print field.

Founded in 1954 in San Francisco to prepare large print textbooks for partially seeing children, NAVH became the pioneer and standard setting agency in the preparation of large type.

Today, those publishers who meet our standards carry the prestigious "Seal of Approval" indicating high quality large print. We are delighted that Thorndike Press is one of the publishers whose titles meet these standards. We are also pleased to recognize the significant contribution Thorndike Press is making in this important and growing field.

Lorraine H. Marchi, L.H.D.
Founder/CEO
NAVH

★ Thorndike Press encompasses the following imprints: Thorndike, Wheeler, Walker and Large Print Press.

# CHAPTER ONE

Dave Kemp sat loosely in the saddle as he let the bay take a blow. It had been two years since he had forked a horse and now, after six miles of steady pounding, he needed a breather, too.

He was a big man, about six-one, and carried his one hundred-ninety pounds with the quick assurance of youth. He closed his eyes and rubbed one hand slowly across his pale forehead. Sweat dripped down his fingers and he wiped it off on the now dusty denim pants. His nostrils twitched with the dust and with the sharp salty smell of the warm horse under him. Then the light fragrance of sage cut through and he grinned. It was good to be going home!

After two years of reading the law in St. Louis, he was coming back. He had prodded the bay up this slope for a long look north, on the off chance he might be able to spot smoke coming from the Circle K one ridge over. No luck.

He would have to swing to the left

around Hawke Ridge before he could see the ranch, and the ribbon of blue that was Broken River.

Lean legs gigged the bay into motion through the ankle-high grass that rolled down to the wagon tracks below. A curious urge pulsed through him and he kicked the bay into a lope. He was eager to get back. He wanted to see his sister, Janie, and the hired hands, and to look over their little spread. His face fell slack for a moment as he thought about the telegram. He would also pay his last respects to his father.

The wire had come on Friday, and the next morning he was on the train headed West. Now he was on the last leg of the long trip, with the little Oregon cowtown of Kings Mountain behind him and less than three miles ahead to the Circle K.

"Dad will be under the Oregon sod by this time," he thought as the bay jogged down to the wagon track. It didn't seem possible. His father was always so strong, so alive, so ready to meet any situation. Now at forty-five he was dead.

Dave had let the bay slow to a fast walk. She was tired, he knew. He had pushed her hard. But three more miles and she could rest all night. He urged her along faster as the unsettling urgency flickered through his mind, faded, then came back.

The road track cut across the flat high country here and shot straight north toward Hawke Ridge. As Dave rode, he went over that confusing day when the telegram had come. Perhaps it was what the wire left unsaid that had prompted his fast trip West.

"Father died this morning after a two-day illness. Doc Bevins has made the arrangements. Josh Hays is administrator for the will. Please come home." It was signed, "Janie."

Dave squinted his hazel-green eyes at the sun as he considered the words again. Janie was nineteen, and competent on horseback or in a kitchen, but she wasn't cut out to manage a two-section spread with six hundred longhorns. The ranch had to be his responsibility. He was twenty-three, tough of lung and limb, and he knew the cattle business from hoof to horn tip. He could work the ranch, or sell out, or find some honest partner. But through it all there was a steady hankering to be a lawyer.

The shadow of an idea that had been darting in and out of his mind for the past few days finally surfaced and he could put it into words.

"Did Janie leave out why Dad died just

to keep me from rushing back here and getting into trouble?"

He let the idea hang there in the warm afternoon sunshine and thought about it. Janie knew he had a quick temper. What if their father had been called out in a fixed gunfight, or cut down by some hired gun, or even bushwhacked? What if the two-day sickness had been lead poisoning? Dave Kemp touched spurs to the flanks of the bay.

He had automatically thought of the pox when Janie said a two-day sickness. Smallpox had killed their mother when he was twelve. Gunshot! The idea stayed with him.

The land of the Circle K was a little better than that of the other two ranches in this end of the valley which had been carved out by the main fork of the Broken River. There were two other finger valleys, the middle fork and Lewis River, which opened into the main valley where Kings Mountain stood. Only the main fork of the river had water in it year-round. It was fed by many springs high in the mountains behind the Kemp ranch. This meant that the Kemp place controlled the only water available in the whole Kings Valley area during a hot, dry summer.

Lloyd Kemp had always been scrupulously

fair about the water, letting more than enough flow through his earthen dams so the ten or twelve other ranchers below had enough water for their stock.

Dave left the wagon tracks of the road and guided the bay up a faint trail over Hawke Ridge. It cut a mile off the wagon road. As he neared the top a jackrabbit scrambled away from a sage and scurried for better cover. The rider's gun hand whipped down and up in one liquid motion and the Colt forty-four snarled. The rabbit spun around and lay still. Dave hefted the six-gun and nodded. The slap of the hickory felt good to his hand. It had been over two years since he had fired the Colt. But once you had learned, learned the way he had, you never lost the touch.

He holstered the forty-four and rode over the ridge top and down toward the wagon trail again. The sun was kicking long shadows from Black Butte ahead of him. Barely two hours of sunlight were left. A goading insistence pushed him on. Soon he would be able to see the chimney smoke from the ranch house. Then the two barns and the sheds and the corrals would show and he could see the whole ranch spread out along the rim of foothills where Broken River tumbled down to the valley floor.

As he guided the bay through a stand of scrub pine, Dave wondered why Janie or Old Charley hadn't met him in town. He had wired his day of arrival. Dave snorted. He was beginning to think like an Eastern dude! The wire was probably still at the telegraph office. Did he think they delivered telegrams on bicycles here the way they did in St. Louis?

Lots of things had changed in Kings Mountain in two years, though. More stores had gone up. There might be a new sheriff, even a mayor of the town now! Must be two hundred people in the community. Even the liveryman was new. He was a tall one, lean as a willow sapling, and bald as a prairie chicken egg. But the man's face was what you noticed. It was thin and gaunt and his eyes were slate gray with flecks of green. Those eyes had chilled Dave; they seemed to speak of death.

Looking back, Dave remembered that the man had seemed surprised when he said he was headed for the Circle K. Or was it just his own imagination?

Most of all now, Dave looked forward to seeing Janie again. From seventeen to nineteen she must have done a lot of growing up. They had been close ever since their mother had died when Janie was eight. Being four years older, a lot of the raising was up to Dave. He remembered it all as he rode. The tomboy stage; how she learned to ride and rope almost as well as he could. That determined little chin and the snub nose that reminded everyone of their mother. Janie wore her hair long and let it fly in the wind instead of braiding it. Her hair was midnight-black and she wore short bangs that framed her face. It would be good to see Janie and to buck up her spirits. He smiled at that. If he knew Janie, she would be the one to keep him on the cheerful side!

Dave narrowed his eyes and thought about the trail. It meandered here, but he remembered it went between the two big boulders ahead. "Rattlesnake rocks" he used to call them.

The brush thinned and the remainder of Hawke Ridge was scattered with boulders and scrub and jack pine. Dave had to slow to pass the big rocks. If he had been riding hard he would have missed the glint of sun on steel which flashed for an instant. It came from the hillside to his right and immediately Dave ducked and slid off the bay on the left side.

He saw the smoke before he heard the whine of the slug over his head. Before the sniper got off a second shot, Dave had dropped behind a rock and whacked the bay into the brush.

The bluish smoke was fading when Dave spotted it, not more than a hundred yards to his right. He had only his six-gun, but Dave knew most bushwhackers were afraid of a fair fight. He began working to the right to close the gap between himself and the gunman. He was midway along Hawke Ridge, and the dwarf pine and sage gave him cover. No more shots were fired as Dave crouched at the same level as the gunman, but closer now. Ahead was a twenty-foot stretch without a boulder or a twig for cover. He found a rock and threw it high and to the side of where the sniper was. As soon as he heard the rock smash into the dry brush, Dave sprinted across the open area ahead of him. He dove and rolled the last few feet and heard one whining rifle slug ram past him.

Dave lay very still behind the rock, trying to quiet the rush of his own breathing. If he had guessed right, the gunman should be moving. A creak of saddle leather brought Dave up and running toward the brush. He made it just as the gunman swung into the saddle some thirty yards down the hill. Dave fired once at the moving target, then clamped his left hand firmly on his right wrist to steady his aim and fired again just as the horse and rider flashed into some pine cover. He missed.

Dave hadn't been close enough to see much of the man's face, but he had been tall, wore black pants and a blue cotton shirt and a high-crowned hat. A description for half the riders on the range!

Dave dropped behind a big boulder and watched the down-trail. Once out of pistol range the rider stopped and slammed three rifle slugs into the protective boulder. The man was riding a big dun-colored horse. He waved his rifle in anger, then turned and rode for town.

When it was clear the rider would not return, Dave ran to his bay and mounted quickly. He kicked the horse into a gallop and broke through the screen of brush and down toward the wagon road.

There was little doubt now; his father's death meant he had inherited trouble! Someone wanted the Circle K enough to kill to get it. Or did they already have it? Had someone run off the hands and taken over the ranch? He urged the bay around the last flush of scrub pine and looked down on Broken River Valley. He strained his eyes, searching the head of the valley, then he relaxed. The barn, the ranch house, everything was still there. But there didn't seem to be any smoke coming from the ranch house. No cooking fire at this time of day? He spurred the bay into motion again. Something down there was wrong!

A few moments later he could see the stock. There were always a number of steers around the buildings this time of year, but now he saw that a hundred head were milling around the barns and house. They should be on the lower range, or in the holding pens.

He rode on but stopped about a half mile from the barns where the wagon road went through some brush and looked over the ranch again. The ranch seemed deserted. There were only two horses in the corral. Nothing in the breaking corral, and no smoke from the chimney.

He swung his mount sharply to the right and moved through the brush and up the ravine to the pine and around to the back of the house where the land began to tilt upward. He tied the bay to a tree and moved cautiously toward the edge of the clearing.

Again, he could see nothing but cattle moving. No fire, no activity in the barns. The sun was beginning to slip over the rimrocks behind him. Dave moved silently as a shadow from the woods and toward the nearest corral. It was empty. He moved on to the back door of the hay barn. The door was open and he slipped inside in one quick motion and dropped to the floor.

There was no answering movement, no roar of six-guns. He rose and searched the area quickly. Near the wide front doors he found a string of forty-four empty casings, as if someone had tried to reload on the run. Now he searched the barn again, carefully, looking for trouble, and sensing disaster. He peered into corners, moved equipment and kicked through stacks of hay.

In the milking stall he found a dead man. One hand showed from a pile of straw. It was Yancy, one of their hands. He had two arrows in his chest and his scalp was gone.

Dave turned his face. He had never seen a scalped man before. He closed his eyes tightly and swallowed hard. "Indians?" he asked in a whisper. There had been no Indian trouble around this part of the country for ten years. Then he turned and ran for the door.

"Janie!" he said, and it was almost a sob.

He stopped suddenly at the barn door. Were the killers still here? He peered around the door at the familiar buildings. Again he could detect no sign of human life, no danger. But he had to be sure. Crouching and with his forty-four in hand, he ran low and fast to the second barn. There was no one inside. The other corral was empty except for two work horses.

No one was here. He straightened and walked toward the ranch house. He didn't want to go inside, but he must. Dave stopped at the kitchen door. Everything looked natural. The curtains waved through the windows. The evening shadows were just starting to climb the pine-log wall. Dave turned the knob and pushed the door open, hard. It swung around and slammed against the wall. Inside everything was in place. Pots of food sat on the stove, but the fire was out. The table was set for four.

Dave checked the sitting room and the dining room. He didn't expect to find her. He took the plank stairs three at a time and stopped at his sister's bedroom door. He knew it was useless, but he knocked. Then he pushed the heavy door open.

Janie Kemp lay on her bed. Bruises mottled her young face, and her long black hair was matted with blood where someone had started to take her scalp. Her face was frozen in horror and agony, even in death.

# CHAPTER TWO

Dave dropped to his knees and hurled a quilt over her, then buried his face in the bedding. He wanted to cry, he needed to scream, but only a low animal moan seeped through his clenched teeth. A rush of memories cascaded over him as he knelt there.

He had no idea how long he stayed on his knees. It was dark when he finally stood, gently covered her face with the quilt and backed out the door.

The living, if any, needed him more. He had to see if anyone had been spared. Numbly Dave found some rags and tied them to a pole with wire, then soaked them with kerosene to make a torch. With it he began searching the rest of the buildings. After ten minutes of looking he found a body near the well house. He did not know the man. There was a bullet hole in his back, and an Indian war club had smashed into the man's skull. Indians again? It didn't add up. The nearest Indians were the Klamath tribe, a placid, friendly group.

They had been content to settle down on their reservation years ago.

Dave quit trying to figure it out. He could do that in the morning. It was nearly half an hour later that he found Old Charley. He was behind the tool shack, and he was still alive. The man was delirious, and Dave soon saw why. Both knees had been shattered with bullets. He had bled a lot, but something else was wrong too.

Dave listened to the whistling, wheezing breath. He had heard that sound before. Someone had crushed Old Charley's throat so he would never talk, so he could never identify the killers. Dave had seen a man once who had been kicked in the throat by a horse. It had taken six months for the crushed throat to mend, and even then the man couldn't speak. He could write though, and he had scratched down what happened. Dave set his jaw grimly. Old Charley couldn't write.

It took Dave over an hour to pick up the ranchhand and carry him into the sitting room. The pain of being moved caused Old Charley to pass out almost at once, and it was a relief to Dave. He laid him in the downstairs bed and cleaned the shattered knees as best he could. They were caked with blood, but the bleeding had stopped.

20

There must have been a lot of lost blood, but the man's pulse was steady and solid.

Dave wrapped the knees with strips of sheets and put a cover over the old man. There was nothing he could do about the smashed throat. Doc Bevins would have to treat Old Charley as soon as possible. Dave pushed the hat back on his head. He had to drive into town tonight with Old Charley. The ranchhand might die before morning with no care. He didn't know how long Charley had been lying out there. And if he did live, Old Charley might, somehow, be able to help identify the killers. At least it was one hope!

Dave rubbed his eyes. There would be little sleep for him tonight. Right now he had the hardest job of all. Dave found a lantern and a pick and shovel and trudged up the path behind the house to the family cemetery. Janie had taken care of the three graves, cutting weeds and grass, keeping the iron grill fence painted black and decorating the graves whenever weather permitted. There was room for three more stones in the little square. He went to his father's new grave and bowed his head for a few moments.

Then Dave dropped the shovel and rammed the pick deep into the earth. The moon was up in a silver crescent to the east, and the cloudless sky showed a billion stars lending their soft light to the lamp glow digging. He paused occasionally to listen and to let his eyes sweep over the shadows around the buildings. No one was there. The killers had been gone a long time.

It took him two hours to dig the grave. He went deep so no marauding coyote could violate it. When he was through he washed his hands near the well and went into the house. The kerosene lamp lighted his way up to his old room next to Janie's, and he found his clothes in the closet. Janie had his room opened up, cleaned out and all ready for him. He put on his best black broadcloth suit and a white shirt and black string tie. He traded his low-cut oxfords for a well-broken-in pair of riding boots.

Then he went to Janie's room. Dave Kemp shuddered slightly when he opened the door. He knew she should be in her best dress, but that was unthinkable now. Gently he wrapped her in a sheet, then in a heavy patchwork quilt. He carried her down the steps, out of the house and up the hill. It was the longest walk of his life.

Two hours later when the mound of dirt was packed down, Dave looked at the grave for several minutes.

"Ashes to ashes, and dust to dust," he said, then blinked his eyes hard. "I'll find them, Janie. Whoever they are, I'll find them!" He turned and went down to the house without looking back.

He changed into denim pants and a wool shirt and found his black work hat. It took him another half hour to locate a team and to harness them to the light wagon. He jousted a mattress from the bunkhouse and laid it in the box of the wagon and threw in three blankets.

Back inside the house, he went to his father's bedroom and looked at the man who lay there. A new hardness came into his face as he thought about the savagery of the attack. Then he picked up the delirious man and carried him to the wagon. Old Charley groaned as Dave laid him gently onto the mattress and covered him with the blankets. Then he tied the cowhand down to the mattress so he couldn't roll off.

Dave made one more trip into the house, this time for the thirty-thirty Winchester rifle. It was in his room in the closet where he had hidden it before he went away. It was clean and ready. He pocketed a box of shells, then blew out the light and locked the door.

Dave looked at the stars. It was almost midnight. He took the livery stable horse and his own big gray and tied them to the back of the wagon, and slid both saddles in beside the mattress. Then he drove the wagon slowly down the trail toward town. It would be a long ride, but it had to be as soft as possible for his passenger.

It was an hour later before the reaction came. Throwing the sod into Janie's grave had started it. There was a finality about it that was so complete, so irrevocable, so unquestionable! Janie was dead. He would never see her again. And Pa was dead!

Never again would he see the slow smile of his father, nor hear the calm, warmth of his voice. Never again would he hear Janie laugh, or see her run to meet him! He thought about it a long time and then he pounded the seat of the wagon with his fist until it was numb.

# CHAPTER THREE

The drive to Kings Mountain took nearly three hours, and there was only one small light burning in the whole town when he arrived. He saw it in the sheriff's office as he drove by on the way to Doc Bevins' house and office. Dave knocked on the door sharply, and in a few seconds it opened. Doc Bevins' balding head jutted through and he nodded at the other man. He held out his hand which Dave grasped.

"Good to have you home, Dave. We need you here."

"Thanks Doc." He nodded at the rig. "I got Old Charley here. He's hurt bad."

"I'll get my pants on," the little man said and turned back into the room. Dave went to the wagon and untied the ropes that had held the patient in place.

The doctor came out before Dave was finished. He carried a narrow wooden door which he put on the mattress beside Charley and gently rolled the cowhand over onto it. Together they carried the broken man inside.

"Gunshot in both knees, Doc, and something's wrong with his throat."

Doc Bevins worked on the knees for the next half hour, taking off the bandages, cleaning the wounds, trying to reshape the splintered kneecaps. Old Charley had remained unconscious since they brought him in. At last the doctor began to talk as he worked.

"Don't know how long you've been in town, Dave. Imagine Janie sent for you. I was 'bout ready to. Things going on in this valley none of us like. And it's got to stop soon or we'll have a range war.

"It happened fast. Not over two months ago things was peaceful around here. Then Hank Contway drifted in."

Dave frowned. "That no-good kid of the Contways we run out of town three years back?"

"That's him, and with his pockets bulging with money. Gold money he says. He bought the Clinton spread below you, and then two weeks later got into a card game with Ray Vanderzanden at the Golden Girl and won his ranch with a full house. Ray called it a cheating hand and went for his gun. Hank shot Ray twice before he cleared leather."

Doc Bevins began washing his hands

and nodded at the patient.

"Knees should be fine, eventually. One might be stiff, but that won't kill him. That throat, though." Doc rubbed his forehead. "That's another kettle of turnip greens. I'll stay up with him tonight, and if he makes it till daylight, reckon he should mend. Not much I can do in there. Some pipes are broken. Just have to let mother nature have her way."

The doctor sat down at the kitchen table and turned, his face flushed. "You know why your pa died?"

Dave could only shake his head.

"Somebody gunned him down, bush-whacked him with a rifle bullet in the back. He was down by the south dam checking the flow of water when the hands heard two shots. By the time they got down there he was unconscious. He lingered on for two days."

Dave turned away, shock, anger, and a need for vengeance flaring across his features. He gently lifted the Colt up and down, up and down in its leather holster. His mind was boiling and a wild, unreasoning rage shook him. It was several minutes before he could speak.

"I . . . I didn't know. Thought as much. Then when I got to the ranch and found

Old Charley and the others, I knew Pa must have been shot."

Doc Bevins looked up quickly. "The others?"

"Yancy's dead, and another cowhand . . . and Janie. . . . I just buried her in the family plot."

"Janie too!?"

Dave nodded. The little doctor stood up and threw the hand towel into the far corner of the room.

"Tell me what you found, Dave."

The young rancher paced the room as he talked. It didn't take long. He described the ranch just as it was when he rode up. When Dave finished, Doc rubbed his stubbled cheeks.

"A woman killer. We haven't had anything like that around here for ten years. Why Janie?"

Dave moved to the door. "I'm gonna find out!"

Doc went outside with him, and watched as Dave untied his gray from the wagon and threw on the saddle.

"I'll send the night livery stable man over for the rig and his horse. You take care of Old Charley." He thought a moment. "Could you put him back in that room where you let drunks sober up? I'd rather no one knew he was still alive." The doctor nodded.

"Dave, go see our new sheriff. Zedicher is his name, and he's honest and good with a gun. I don't want you taking on a batch of bushwhackers alone."

"My next stop. He asleep in the office?" Dave got a confirming nod as he finished cinching up the saddle. He jammed the Winchester into the boot and put the box of cartridges into the saddlebag. A wave to the doctor and Dave swung up and trotted the horse down the street toward the sheriff's office.

Kings Mountain was a typical cowtown in the Northwest. False front buildings, some of clapboard, some made of chinked logs. There was one long block of businesses on both sides of the street, a scattering of houses, a schoolhouse and one church, and the little Kings County courthouse.

The sheriff's office nestled beside the bank which was the only brick structure in town. The Oregon Trust and Security Bank hadn't been robbed in fifteen years. Dave swung off the gray and wrapped the reins around the rail, vaulted it and stepped lightly onto the rough plank porch of the lawman's office. There was no movement on the street. He listened at the door and heard only a light snore. Dave knocked sharply and heard the snore change key. He pounded on the door with his hand and set the latch to rattling. Then boots hit the floor.

"I'm coming, don't break it down!" a voice inside growled.

When the door opened it was dark inside, and no one stood at the opening. Then a six-gun jammed into Dave's ribs as a man moved quickly and kicked the door aside.

Dave put up his hands. "Dave Kemp, Sheriff. We've never met."

The six-gun dropped an inch, a match flared and the sulphur stung Dave's nose as the flame wheeled close to his face. There was a grunt of satisfaction and the match floated through the dark room to the lamp, which blossomed into a pale yellow light.

"Come on in, Kemp. Been expecting you." The voice was neutral.

Dave moved inside and looked at the man with the badge. He was just over six feet, and muscled hard and firm. His shoulders were a yard wide and a three-inch leather belt cinched a narrow waist. The full moustache bristled below a square-cut nose and thin mouth. Dark hair drooped around the corners of huge ears.

The sheriff had buckled on his gunbelt as Dave looked him over. Now he slouched in his chair behind the desk.

"Have you found the man who killed my pa, yet?"

Luke Zedicher uncoiled from the chair in a fraction of a second, his large hands hovering at half mast in front of him, his face hard and cold. Dave immediately regretted the inference. He couldn't afford to get off on the wrong foot with the new law.

Zedicher dropped his hands slowly and relaxed his whole frame as a slow grin began to crawl around his eyes, and break out over his mouth.

"Fact is, I haven't, Kemp. They told me you had the fastest mouth in the county. Now I see why."

"Look, Sheriff. I didn't come here to get yahooed. I got a perfect right to . . ."

"Hold it, Kemp! Get this straight! I am the law in Kings County. I run things and keep the peace. Any troublemaker comes in, I shuck him of his hardware and ride him out of town." He paused and the hint of the smile flirted with his eyes. "Besides I don't take kindly to being rousted out of bed in the middle of the night."

Hot words rushed into Dave's mouth but he caught himself. He needed this lawman's help. He held his tongue with a great effort and saw the grin in the lawman's eyes grow. Dave beat down his anger savagely, and when he spoke it was in a low, controlled voice.

"Sheriff, I'm reporting the murder of two of my hands, a brutal attack on a third, and the assault and murder of my sister, Janie Kemp."

Sheriff Zedicher's eyes froze for a moment and his hands went to his gunbelt. He resettled the forty-four at his right hip and reached for his highcrowned, gray Stetson. He grabbed a denim jacket and pointed out the door. A nod of his head aimed them at the livery stable.

While the sheriff saddled a broad-chested black, Dave told the night stable man to pick up the rented horse and saddle and hold his team and wagon for him.

"Soon as the saloon opens, see if you can find me three good cowhands and send them out to the Circle K. Send me some good men and not some grubline riders, and I'll make it worth your while." The tall, bald man nodded.

The sheriff was ready to move, and Dave saw he had a saddle packed and ready for a long trail. They kicked the horses into a lope out the Middle Fork Road that headed north.

# CHAPTER FOUR

During the two-hour ride to the Circle K, Dave told the sheriff exactly what he found hours earlier when he rode into the ranch. He also covered the bushwhacking attempt on himself, and described the man and horse as well as he could. So far that was the only evidence they had of any kind.

The sheriff's eyes narrowed occasionally during the narrative, and Dave knew he would have to repeat nothing, explain nothing.

"The arrows, did you save them?"

"Sure. They had two different markings."

"Saw something like this in Arizona, few years back."

"Renegade Indians?"

"What do you think?"

Dave shook his head. "Not what the Klamaths would do, even renegades. They would want beef and horses, and they would have carried off any women."

The sheriff nodded. "This sounds like a

33

clumsy try to cover up three murders. Find any tracks?"

"Didn't look."

"And the trail will be eighteen to twenty-four hours old by now?"

"Yep."

They pushed their horses harder then, and arrived at the ranch just before dawn sent crimson streamers into the morning clouds over the range of hills to the east. Everything was as it had been. Dave rounded up the loose stock into the south meadow and came back to the well. The sheriff had taken a drink and offered the dipper to Dave. Then they looked at the two bodies.

"Forget about Indians. This arrow has dried blood marks halfway up the shaft. That other one had the feathers broken off long time ago. And no Indian worth his knife would scalp anyone like that was done."

Together they checked the area near the house for any sign of riders. There were no tracks except for the ones Dave had made the evening before. The men mounted again and rode a quarter of a mile down the town road, then split and took opposite directions, circling the ranch buildings to look for tracks. Dave had gone only a few hundred yards off the road when he leaned out of his saddle, staring at the ground. He called the sheriff.

"Three horses, all shod," he said when the lawman rode up. "They came in at a walk, but didn't come back this way."

It was slow, neck-wrenching work as the two riders followed the old trail. It went roughly parallel to the road, then wound around the barns and behind the corral. Three horses had been tied there for some time. But the jumble of tracks from the stock made trying to follow the horses any farther impossible.

"Let's circle the buildings again, closer in," Dave said. "We should be able to pick up their tracks going out." Half an hour later Dave heard the sheriff whoop from behind the house, and Dave rode over. Zedicher wiped his forehead with his sleeve and pointed toward the mountains behind him.

"Two of them went up here. I don't know how far, or if they stayed, but they sure left in a hurry."

Dave read the sign and agreed. The soft ground had been cut up by the eight hooves.

"You circle the other way from here, Kemp, and try to pick up the other rider.

I'll backtrack these and see what I can find."

"Sheriff, I was raised here. I can find anybody up there in half the time you could."

The sheriff pointed toward town. There was a small plume of dust moving slowly across the valley from Hawke Ridge. "You're going to have company, probably your new hands."

Dave hesitated, then nodded and rode back toward the barn. He unsaddled his horse and went to work. Suddenly he realized he was hungry. He hadn't eaten since noon the day before at the stage stop down from Kings Mountain. There should be some eggs and bacon left in the well house cooler. He started for the well and thought of the riders. They might want some chow, too, before starting work.

He had the eggs frying on a cook fire in the kitchen wood range when he saw the three riders come into the yard and dismount. He went to the door and called to them, and they turned quickly, hands near gunbutts. Most cowhands didn't pack guns around there, and Dave wondered about it. He went to meet them and was about thirty feet away when he noticed the three were standing straddle-legged, hands poised.

"Hold it right there, Kemp. Not a step farther! What you doin' on my land?"

Dave Kemp squinted into the sun to see the man talking. He was the shortest of the three, not over five-foot-six, and he carried two guns hung low like some dime-novel desperado. His hands flared above the iron, fingers flexing slightly in anticipation.

"This is the Circle K, the Kemp ranch," Dave said. "It's mine. What are you doing here?"

"Playing games, Kemp. You want to play?" With the invitation the man's hand flashed down, a gun glued to his fingers and the weapon swept up and fired. Stones sprayed an inch to the right of Dave's foot.

The man dropped the smoking forty-five back into its leather home.

"Want to play games, Kemp? Draw on me. Go ahead, draw! Slow man is out." He laughed a high chuckle. "Way out — he's dead!"

Dave had to think back three years. This was the same kid with the gun they had run out of the valley. Hank Contway — older, smarter, and his gun much faster.

"Contway, I heard you were back. You're still a punk kid."

Contway drew again and chipped dust half an inch at the side of Dave's other foot. His face was sun-red now, his eyes burning.

"Don't you ever call me that again, Kemp, or I'll gun you down! You hear!" Then suddenly his attitude changed, and he slid the gun back into leather.

"Look, Kemp. No reason we can't be friends. Everything I'm doin' is legal and proper. This is my ranch, and I'm asking you to move on."

"What you talking about?"

The smaller man walked toward Kemp, a grin splitting his face under dark, un-smiling eyes. He held out a piece of paper.

"Take a look, Kemp. Take a close look!"

Then Dave was staring at an official bill of sale, registered and notarized and legal. At the bottom was the stubborn scrawl of his father's hand. It had to be his pa's writing, only his pa made "o's" that looked like "e's". Dave reached for the paper.

"Don't touch, saddle tramp!" Contway barked. "Get your horse and gear and be off my ranch in ten minutes!"

# CHAPTER FIVE

Dave Kemp could only stare at the piece of paper. He didn't see the other man slide behind him. Then two thick arms strapped around him, pinning his own arms to his sides in a powerful bear hug. Dave lashed backwards with a boot but it found no bone.

Hank Contway tucked the bill of sale paper in his pocket and moved closer.

"You're a little too feisty for your own good, big man. I best calm you down a turn." Contway slashed a fist at Dave's jaw that rocketed his head back onto his shoulders. Then, as the other man held Dave, Contway smashed again and again into his face and midsection.

At last he stood back. "You went soft, Dave, back there with all those law books," he said. "You don't look in too good a shape right now, and that eye is almost closed. Might as well finish the job." He swung again and Dave, numbed now to the pain, hardly felt the knuckles dig into his cheek and eye.

On signal the other man released his arms, and Contway moved in again. "I like to see a man fall when I hit him, drifter." Dave saw the fist flailing out of the distance, felt it touch his chin. It didn't hurt at all! But he was falling and rolling in the dust. Contway waited for him to stagger up.

"Like I said, drifter, you get back on your horse and hightail it out of here. We got no room for landless cowpokes in this country."

Hank drove in again. He slashed Dave's head and sent him sprawling into the dust. This time he stepped up and drove his boot into Dave's side. The fallen man rolled over on his back in agony as his kidney screamed and his stomach retched. He couldn't stand up now, he couldn't even turn over. He lay there with his knees drawn up as the brutal pains stabbed again and again and again.

Dave barely heard the rifle shot, but Hank's white, high-crowned Stetson leaped off his head and fell behind him. Almost at the same time the voice came from up the slope.

"Hold it down there! The man who moves gets shot! Contway, you and your two gunslicks drop your iron." There was a moment of hesitation. Another rifle slug ripped dust between the feet of one of the gunmen. "Drop them now!" It was a voice that demanded obedience.

The three dropped their gunbelts into the dirt and stood looking uphill. Dave closed his eyes as a wave of darkness passed over him and he shivered against it. He couldn't pass out, not now! He opened his eye and struggled up on one elbow and watched the sheriff walk down the hill. The rifle held at the hip centered on the trio and the lawman's eyes never left Contway's face. He stopped beside Dave and without looking down spoke.

"What's this about?"

Dave tried to talk, but the dirt in his mouth and the nausea were too much. He shook his head.

"I'll be glad to tell you, Sheriff," Contway said. "Cat got his tongue you might say."

"Talk, Contway, but stay right there."

"I got a bill of sale to this place. His old man signed it over to me a few days before he died. So I want you to throw this here saddle tramp off my land!"

"Let's see the paper," the sheriff said. Contway brought it over and the sheriff studied it. Then he knelt and gave it to

Dave, but the rifle was still ready. "Is that your pa's writing?" the sheriff asked.

Dave tried to focus his eyes on it, then realized he had to worry about seeing with only his right eye. At last he got it cleared so he could read the paper. The signature looked like it could be his pa's. Dave swallowed and tried to sit up a little more, then he found the words and wheezed them out.

"Must be forged!"

"What do you mean, forged?" Contway bellowed. "I bought this property fair and square! Used my hard-earned gold-digging money for it. He's a liar if he says that ain't his pa's signature!"

"Circuit court judge can decide that," the sheriff said. "He'll be around in a couple of weeks."

"Still my ranch?" Dave whispered.

"Far as I'm concerned," the sheriff said.

"File complaint against Contway," Dave said, barely able to whisper. "Assault and battery."

Sheriff Zedicher shook his head. "That's Eastern law, son. Judge would laugh you out of court unless you were busted up some." He rubbed his chin looking at Contway. "You might call it attempted murder, then you might have a case."

"What you trying to do, Sheriff?" Contway screamed.

"You take my advice, gunslick. You pick up your iron over there and mount up and ride out of here. Don't let me catch you pounding on anybody else in this county or I'll personally horsewhip you and throw you into Broken River with a rock around your neck. Now vamoose!"

The three men claimed their revolvers sullenly and mounted up. Only the rifle aimed in their direction kept them in motion.

When they were gone the sheriff brought a pail of water from the well house so Dave could wash his face and rinse out his mouth. His breath was coming easier now, and the pain was only a steady roar through his brain, not a flood tide. He could begin to talk again, and after another ten minutes he sat up. His left eye was still closed and would stay that way for a day or two.

The sheriff hunkered down and looked at Dave again.

"You'll live. Saw that kick you took. Dirty trick." The sheriff looked away, closing the matter. He looked uphill. "Didn't find much up that trail. It petered out on some shale. The riders might have kept on going up and over the ridge, or cut back down across the shale. Didn't think it was important enough to worry about. Then I heard those shots and I got back down here."

"Glad you did," Dave said. His voice was stronger now. "Who were the two side-winders with Contway?"

"The Larchmont brothers, a pair of gunslicks from Arizona. Been with Contway since he came back. He never goes very far without them. First handles are Bill and Curley."

"I'll remember them," Dave said. He felt better and drank a little water. It hit his stomach like raw whiskey, but it stayed down. He tried to stand up and Zedicher steadied him. Dave's legs were made of marsh grass and willow leaves, but at last he firmed them and made them hold him straight. It was a long walk to the kitchen.

Dave sat in a straight chair while the sheriff finished cooking the eggs and bacon.

The sun was two hours old before they had eaten. By this time Dave was starting to hurt. He wasn't numb anymore and he could walk, but the pounding he had taken was showing. After they ate, the sheriff took a paper out of his pocket.

"What about his bill of sale?"

Dave shook his head. "Dad wouldn't sell without at least talking it over with Janie and me." Dave looked at the document. "It's dated July 1. When did Pa get shot?"

The sheriff shook his head. "About two weeks ago, I guess. I could look it up."

"Why would a man sell his ranch, then get himself bushwhacked? Might get bushwhacked if he didn't sell — seems more logical. Then the bill of sale shows up, pre-dated to make it all look legal. They got Janie and the hands and they tried to get me. Then they decided to work the phony bill of sale!"

"You think Contway killed your pa and sister?"

Dave shook his head. "I don't know. Looks that way, but that's too obvious. In St. Louis I learned the obvious isn't necessarily always true."

"Your pa owe anybody money?"

"Ranch usually made money."

The sheriff rubbed the stubble on his chin. "And your pa never was a big loser at the Golden Girl tables?"

"He played now and then, but he wasn't a big gambler."

The sheriff nodded as if he knew that were so.

"I'm going to contest that bill of sale. I'll be in town later to sign a complaint. Would it do any good to charge Contway with attempted murder?"

"No. You didn't get busted up none, and Contway would have two witnesses to say you started the ruckus."

Dave stood up and winced at the various aches and pains that pounded through his chest and side and head.

"You got time to help me do some digging, Sheriff?" Dave asked. "We need two more graves."

When the last shovel of dirt was packed on the second grave and the wooden markers were pounded in, the sun was directly overhead. Three wranglers had come about an hour before and Dave had them at work sorting out the stock and getting it herded back where it belonged. They still hadn't found the two milk cows. Dave knew he should take a long ride around the ranch to see what needed to be done. But that would have to wait. First he had to get to town and get some questions answered. He found the cowhand he had recognized and called to him from the kitchen. The sheriff was out hunting the other tracks they had missed that morning.

When the wrangler came into the kitchen, Dave shook his hand and asked him to sit down. "Your name is Sanders, isn't it? Jim Sanders?" The wiry man with a closely cropped moustache and thinning hair nodded. He was about thirty and Dave recognized him as a top hand who had been punching cattle in the valley for the past ten years.

"Jim, I need a foreman here," Dave said. "Somebody who can run the place while I'm gone, take care of things, and maybe even throw a little lead if he has to. Got a six-gun?"

"In the bunkhouse."

"From now on, wear it. I had some trouble this morning with Hank Contway. He might be back. If you want to ramrod this spread I'll give you found and forty-five dollars a month. Fair enough? Tell the hands they get thirty dollars and found."

"Fair enough," Jim said, the crinkling edge of a smile breaking across his serious face.

"Jim, you know this cattle business as well as I do. Take a ride and see what needs to be done with the corrals, the top pens, the two dams, the sluice gates and the buildings."

The new foreman nodded. He wore a

smile and his shoulders swung back just a little as he turned and walked toward the barn.

The sheriff rode into the yard and slid off at the well house. "Checked that other set of prints," he said. "They started back toward town, but I lost them where some steers had crossed. 'Bout time I start back to town."

Dave knew he should be going in soon, too. Then he remembered his Western manners. "Noontime, Sheriff. You want something to eat? One of the hands is working on a stew."

The sheriff laughed. "Think I'll pass. I've seen that line-camp stew before! I'll stick with the jerky in my bags." He handed Dave his saddle canteen. "Could use some fresh water, though."

Dave filled the big canteen, having trouble hitting the opening with his one-eyed aim. When it was filled he tossed it back.

"I should be in town this evening. Way I feel I might stay over. Thanks for the help today."

The big man touched his hat brim, mounted up and trotted the black toward the town road.

Dave went back to the kitchen where the

coolness of the house flooded over him and his eye blurred for a moment, and it was only then that he realized he hadn't had any sleep for a day and a half. He needed a few hours before he went into town. Had to be thinking straight then — and maybe shooting straight.

Dave lay down on the divan in the sitting room. His side hurt more now, and his face was as torn up as a pair of old chaps. He sat up and went to the kitchen for the arnica and swabbed it on the bruises. Then he washed out the cuts with glycerin and taped on three small court plasters. The effort exhausted him. He went back, rubber-legged, to the divan, his mind fuzzy. He lay down and was asleep almost at once.

Dave awoke with a start. Some noise? But what? Then it came again and he realized it was someone knocking on the kitchen door. His mind slowly cleared and he sat up.

"Yeah?"

"Mr. Kemp?"

"Coming." He rubbed his face gently with his hands and winced. It would be two or three days before he felt right. He groaned as he stood. Jim Sanders waited at the door.

"Got a count on the horses, fourteen in

49

all," Sanders explained. "Then we took a ride around. Looks like the spring calves ain't been branded. Getting long into July. Shoulda been done."

Dave nodded. "Thanks, Jim. Make a list of things to do. We'll go over it tomorrow. Right now I've got to get into town to see the banker. I'll be back tomorrow."

"You want me to ride shotgun?"

"Thanks, Jim, I'll be fine." Sanders left and Dave looked at the kitchen clock. Jim must have set it. It said four-thirty. Dave washed again, stripping to the waist and doing the job in cold water. Then he began to shave. It had been more than two days, and with cold water and a straight razor, it made the most painful shave of his life. He pulled on a clean flannel shirt and knotted a kerchief around his throat.

He looked for the bank account book his pa had kept. It was in the usual place, right under the match box on the top kitchen shelf. The last entry was made the middle of June and it showed a balance of over two thousand dollars. Dave whistled. Usually his pa never kept that much money in the bank. He slipped the book in his pocket and went out to saddle the gray.

# CHAPTER SIX

During the long, slow ride to town, Dave did some thinking. Who would go after the Circle K? His lawyer's mind went to work. Who was the most obvious choice? Hank Contway. But was Contway stupid enough to draw so much attention to himself, then go out and kill two men and a woman, and the next day show up with a bill of sale that might be forged? He lifted the flat-crowned hat off his head and resettled it. Hank *might* be that dumb, and wild stupid, but Dave didn't think so.

From what Doc Bevins said, the whole valley seemed caught up in it somehow, yet it had started when Hank Contway came back to Kings Mountain.

At this point a good lawyer would ask a lot of questions, get all of the answers he could and begin to research. That was his first job. And it would start at the bank. If anything were awry with his pa's account, the banker would know about it. The bank would be closed by the time he got there, but he could go to the Archer house. The

51

Archers and Kemps had been family friends for twenty years. Lyle Archer and Dave's pa came to the valley about the same time, back when there weren't more than two dozen souls in the whole area.

Evening cooking smokes plumed into the still warm afternoon air as Dave tied up his horse at the white picket fence and went up the flagstone walk to one of the best houses in town. Lyle Archer had built the house twenty years ago, and it was rock-solid, practical, and still one of the best houses in town.

Dave knocked and almost at once the door edged open. Standing there was Susannah Archer, and Dave felt a twinge deep in his chest that he had thought was dead and gone.

"Hello, Sue."

"Hello, Dave. I . . . I guess you want to see my uncle." She turned and fled, leaving Dave standing there in the entranceway. That didn't seem at all the way a girl should act, he thought, especially one who had attended a San Francisco finishing school.

Sue looked the same — wonderful! with long brown hair and pert bangs that reminded him of Janie's. But the sparkle was gone from her eyes and her voice was strange, almost . . . frightened.

Lyle Archer rolled around the doorjamb at full throttle and held out a meaty hand, smothering Dave with an outburst of welcome.

"Come in, Dave, come in, boy! Don't know what got into Susie, running off that way. Overfinished, maybe!" He chuckled.

The sitting room was almost as it had been two years ago. Dave had seen it often then at parties and meetings, and courting.

Archer motioned him into an overstuffed chair.

"Dave, we're all very sorry about your pa. Just nothing we could do." He turned around, and the somber mood dissolved.

"Dave Kemp, the traveler! How are you? Say, let's have some brandy to wash the dust out of your throat." He raised his voice as he looked back at the door. "Helen! Helen, bring us some brandy glasses!" he bellowed.

Lyle Archer hadn't changed at all, Dave decided. Still the hearty host, a stout man who was given to fat, and who liked to bluster his way through things rather than use the cold fist of his power in the community, a power which was both strong and well defined.

He owned half the town, literally. Main Street was the dividing line, and he built on his half the shops along the north side of Main Street, and the bank, two saloons, and the hotel. He let anyone who wanted to build on the other side of the street. It had been a smart move and as ranchers came and the cowtown grew, the banker prospered.

Sue, not her aunt, brought the glasses and the brandy. She set them down without looking at Dave and left the room.

"Good to have you back, Dave!" Archer boomed. "Must have been two years. Get finished reading law? Always can use another good lawyer in a town this size. Say Dave, looks like you hurt your eye."

Dave didn't know what to expect, surely not this bubbling, "all's well" attitude. He realized he hadn't answered the question.

"My eye? Oh, fell off my horse into some brush." He paused. "About the law. I've read enough to practice here in Oregon. I was thinking about staying in Missouri before the wire came."

The hand on the brandy bottle shook slightly, then firmed as it poured two stemware glasses a quarter full.

"Tragedy! Tragedy! We go along peaceful here for years, then the wild instincts of our fellow men rise to the surface and stark terror breaks out." Archer paused and glanced up. "I hope your sister Janie didn't take his death too hard."

Dave stiffened visibly at the words, and the banker noticed.

"Did I say anything out of place?" Archer asked.

The hardness came back into Dave's face and his mouth tensed. "I buried Janie last night, Mr. Archer. She and two of my hands were killed yesterday."

Dave watched the reaction intently.

"Oh, no! Not another Kemp murdered! This is outrageous! Have you told Sheriff Zedicher? Horrible, horrible." The big man shook his head and stared into the brandy. He swirled it once, twice and then drank. "How can we stop it all?"

Dave was surprised at the fierceness of the banker's reaction.

"And a woman killing! Outrageous. We haven't had anything like that around here for ten years."

Dave was puzzled. He looked at the banker. "That's the second time I've heard about a woman-killing ten years ago. I don't remember it. I was fourteen at the time."

Archer squirmed in his chair and

55

drained the last drops of the brandy. Then he looked at Dave and his face paled a little. "Why I thought you knew, Dave. It was your mother."

"But she died of the pox!"

"Dave, that's what we told everyone it was. You were off on a trail drive to the railhead. We got word to your pa and he came back. Remember when he left the drive? Sheriff thought we could dig out the killer easier if we hushed it up, and with the epidemic of pox right then . . . we said it was the pox."

The banker shook his head. "Sorry I had to be the one to tell you. Thought your pa had told you before now. I always thought it was some grub-line rider passing through and tried to get smart with your ma. Your pa never gave up. Came to see me with some wild story he heard about a year ago. He thought it was somebody here in town. Nothing came of it. New sheriff must have read about it in his back reports. Doc Bevins is the only other one who knows, I guess."

Dave put the brandy glass down suddenly. His mother murdered, too? And ten years ago. Did it have anything to do with the other killings of his family?

Lyle Archer stood and walked around

the room. "Sorry I was the one who told you. Sorry! We've shocked each other tonight. I'm truly sorry." He paused, looking down at the younger man. "Dave, if there's anything I can do . . ."

Dave stood then, his mind awhirl. But why would Lyle Archer lie about anything, and especially something like this? He'd ask Doc and the sheriff. Then he remembered why he came to see the banker.

"Mr. Archer, what about pa's account at the bank? I found this book. Is it up to date?"

The banker took the account book Dave produced and scanned it.

"Looks to be all in order. Yes, that would be the balance." Then he paused. "This is probably profit from the last cattle roundup. Your pa was a smart cattleman. Borrowed some money a year ago to bring in some Texas cattle. Drove them up here. Wanted some new breeding stock to build up his herd. Then he put in another earthen dam that saved his whole ranch last year when it was so dry." The banker paused again. "Seems there was something else." He snapped his fingers.

"Of course. Latter part of June your pa deposited almost five thousand dollars in cash, and gold. Said he didn't have his

57

account book with him, but he'd bring it in. I remembered the amount because it seemed so large. I joked with him about selling the ranch. So we should add that figure to your account."

Dave nodded. His mind was churning again. Money from the sale of the ranch? Now why did the banker say that? On a hunch he reached into his shirt pocket and took out the bill of sale the sheriff had left with him.

"Mr. Archer, where could a man get a form like this?"

The banker looked at it, surprise tinging his face. "Most banks have this form. Lawyers should have them. But we use a different type. I didn't know your ranch had been sold."

"It wasn't sold."

"But the signature?"

"That's what I'm working on. The bill of sale is made out to Hank Contway, and it's dated July 1, very close to the time Pa died. From what you've said, he spent too much money improving the ranch to want to sell it."

"That's a point, yes." The eyes of the banker no longer sparkled.

Dave nodded. "I'll be in tomorrow to sign any papers I need to for Pa's obligations at the bank. Just wanted to tell you I'll be running the Circle K from now on."

Dave left the banker a few minutes later. He mounted and had ridden half a block when a boy scurried out from the shadows of early evening and called to him.

"Mr. Kemp?"

Dave reined in and nodded.

"Got a message." The boy gave Dave a light-blue envelope and ran back the way he had come. Dave palmed the envelope and rode on. Too many people were interested in his movements. He didn't want to accommodate someone ready with a shotgun. He tied up at the Beefsteak House across from the hotel and opened the envelope. There was a note inside and Dave read it in the glow of the lamplight.

"Must see you. Must talk! Meet me at the window of my room as soon as it gets dark." It was signed with a large "S". "S" for Sue Archer. And he knew where her room was. They had planned to elope from that window more than two years ago. He had known Sue for five years — ever since she had been orphaned when her parents died in a house fire in San Francisco. Lyle Archer was her closest relative and the childless couple had accepted her gratefully.

Dave looked at the sky. It wasn't full

dark yet, wouldn't be for half an hour, so Dave moved into the restaurant. He ordered a rare steak with potatoes and green beans and had two cups of coffee before the cook had seared the beef on the outside and sent it to him still sizzling. When Dave came out of the cafe it was dark, with a few clouds flying past a quarter moon. He left his horse where it was and ambled down the block to the alley. When he edged into the darkness he ran through the alley, emerging near the livery stables and walked quickly another block before he melted into the shrubs near the church. He waited five minutes, until he was sure no one had followed him.

Dave hurried then to the Archer house. He vaulted the low fence and moved silently up to Sue's window. A tap on the pane brought an immediate response as slender arms pushed up on the window frame. It raised noiselessly and Sue Archer leaned out. She sat waist high to Dave and he wanted to touch her.

She reached out and took his hand, her eyes brimmed with tears until she brushed them away.

"Oh, Dave, I was so afraid you wouldn't come. After the way I ran away from you tonight, and it's been so long . . . and you've been hurt . . . and those marks on your face, and your eye . . . I wanted you to come back so very much!"

Dave patted her hand. He didn't know what to say. He felt as if he had three left feet when he stood near this lovely girl.

"Don't cry. Susie, don't cry. I'm back. I was the one who ran away before!"

"Oh, Dave, I'm terrified. I know something I shouldn't. I think I know who killed your father!"

# CHAPTER SEVEN

"What did you say, Sue?"

"I think I know who killed your father."

Dave stared at her in the dim light. Her eyes were flooding with tears again and the soft skin seemed tight and pale across her cheeks. Her lips quivered as she reached for him and held him tightly.

"I'm so frightened I can hardly move!"

There was a jangle of harness and creak of leather and wood as a buggy whirled past the house. Dave looked toward the street.

"There's no place to talk except in here," Sue said. "Come in quickly."

Dave knew it was true. He jumped up and squirmed through the window head first, and sat on the floor where he landed until Sue had pulled the shades and turned up the lamp.

They stood close together and Sue spoke in a low voice. "It was just a day or two before your father was shot," she said. "I went down to the livery stable to pick up a buggy so I could go out to see Mrs. Hanson at her farm. I waited near the front of the place and I could hear three men talking. Uncle Lyle told me the rig would be ready, and I was impatient. Usually I don't go inside the livery stable, but I was late, and so I walked to that little office they have about halfway back.

"I was just outside when I heard an angry man's voice. It said something like 'You'll pay me that twenty dollars you owe me right now or we'll settle it with knuckles.' The other man's voice was low and smooth and satin-silk. I'll never forget what he said. That man said: 'I'll pay you your twenty dollars in two or three days. Soon as I get this hombre in my sights I'll bring you the cash. I'm getting a hundred dollars for a little target practice on Lloyd Kemp.' "

Suddenly Dave was aware that he had been holding her by the shoulders and his hands had been getting tighter and tighter.

"Dave, your hands!"

He let go of her and banged his fist into his hand and felt his temper surging away. He wanted to dive through the window and run to the livery stable and haul out the man with the low voice and pistol whip him down to his spurs!

But he found the strength to hold his temper and he tensed as footsteps came toward the door of Sue's room. They stopped and Lyle Archer's voice boomed through the oak.

"Sue Ann, supper is almost ready."

"All right, I'll be right there."

The steps went the other way this time, and Sue continued. "As soon as I heard the man in the livery stable say that, I ran out to the front of the place and waited a few seconds. Then I yelled loud for somebody to get my rig. I stayed right there at the front doors and in a minute the tall man with the bald head came out. I told him I wanted my rig readied and that he was late. I scolded him good, then. I was frightened. He didn't say a word, just looked at me, got my rig and waved me on. So I'm not sure if he was the one talking or if he knew that I heard."

"Have you seen him around here since?"

"Oh, no!"

"Then you're probably safe. Just don't go near that livery barn and don't go wandering around town alone." He reached up and wiped the tears that had eddied down from her frightened brown eyes.

"You've given me a place to start. Now I can find my pa's killer." He paused and looked at her. "Does Josh Mankin still have his law office next to the freight depot?"

She said yes, and looked at him and smiled, then bit her lip. Her eyes looked almost like the laughing brown sparklers they used to be. "Dave, I think you'd better go now. After all, this is my bedroom."

He smiled at her as she turned the lamp down low and he went through the window quickly and knelt on the dew-laden grass, watching, listening. Then he stood, and ran silently back to the street. He walked purposefully now, toward the office of the lawyer. Josh should know what was happening. He worked for everyone in town.

A light still burned in the lawyer's window when Dave came up. He knocked on the door.

"Yes? . . . I was about to close," Josh said. The door swung farther open and the light showed Dave's face. "Dave Kemp! Come in! Heard you were back." It was genuine enthusiasm. Dave slid into the room quickly and closed the door.

"Don't want to make a target of myself again, Josh."

Josh nodded. He was a compactly built man with a full head of hair which he wore longer than the fashion; he was meticulously clean shaven, and dressed like a preacher in suit and vest, string tie and white shirt.

"I talked to the sheriff this afternoon,"

65

Josh said. "I . . . I heard about Janie. She hadn't exactly promised me, but I had been courting." He turned away and rubbed his hand over his face. When he turned back he was composed.

"Anything, Dave! I'll do anything! I had never understood a lynch mob before. Now I do! I could be a one-man lynch mob and laugh all the way to the tree! Just show me the man who did that to Janie, and I'll . . . I'll tear his heart out with my bare hands!"

Josh slumped to his desk chair and tears began streaming down his cheeks. He didn't sob or make a sound, but the tears kept coming.

Dave looked away, then sat down in the other chair near the desk. "I know what you mean, how you feel. I've got a triple score to settle! So we whip them, Josh, we whip them with brains! What can you tell me? What's been happening around here? What's going on? Did Pa make any bad enemies? Did anyone lose cattle last summer in that dry spell? Where's the first place to start, Josh?"

Josh sat up and wiped his eyes and went to a stand near the back where he washed his face. When he came back he had a whiskey bottle and two cups. Josh Mankin began to talk, and he answered every question Dave had asked. When he was done most of the lamps along Main Street had been blown out, and only the saloon and the sheriff's office were lighted.

As they talked they analyzed every facet, but they could find no enemy ready to blow a hole in Lloyd Kemp. They could determine no large losses of cattle or money from the management of the flow of the Broken River water. They could pinpoint no slow-growing problems that could erupt into a range war. Josh knew of no big developments in the valley, he was certain no gold had been discovered here as it had in California. Gently Dave probed about Hank Contway.

"Contway came back to town two or three months ago," Josh answered. "Seemed to have lots of money. Fact he asked me to write out a bill of sale for the Clinton ranch. I did and notarized it and filed it for him at the courthouse. Also wanted me to transfer the deed to the Ray Vanderzanden ranch, but I told him he'd better do that himself."

"You and Contway about the same age, Josh?"

"He's two years younger. I'm twenty-nine now. No, no, he's lots younger. He can't be over twenty or twenty-one."

Josh filled his cup again. In another half hour he would pass out at his desk, Dave decided. "You have a sleep, Josh. Let's talk some more tomorrow. I'm going over to the hotel for some shut-eye myself."

Dave picked up his hat and snapped the night lock on the door as he went out.

He headed for the sheriff's office through the deserted streets.

The sheriff had two lamps burning when Dave arrived. The lawman was struggling with a stack of paper work, wanted posters and pencils with broken leads. He dropped his pencil when Dave came in, evidently glad for a break.

"Still in one piece, I see, Kemp."

"So far. Where do those Larchmont boys hang out in town?"

Luke Zedicher leaned back in his chair and yawned, then stretched both hands toward the beamed ceiling.

"Usually in a saloon, or at the tables of the Golden Girl." He paused, staring at the lamp. "Seems I've seen them coming out of the livery stable too, time or so. Guess they bed down in there and save the fifty cents for a hotel room."

"Buddies with the night livery man, then?"

68

"Figures. He's a hardcase name of Slade Jackson."

"Hardcase? He wanted anywhere?"

"Figures, but I ain't got a wanted notice on him yet. Been here about six months. Drifted in here from California, way I hear. Said he found a big nugget in a creek bed and it scared the hair off his head. Not a friendly type, a loner." He paused and looked directly at Kemp. "You got anything yet?"

"Nope. Talked to Josh Mankin. He's broke up 'bout Janie."

Neither man said anything for a moment. Dave turned toward the door and the sheriff sighed and picked up the pencil again. "I'll keep in touch, Sheriff," Dave said.

"I'm hopin' you do, Kemp!"

Dave went out the door and headed for the hotel. The Kings Hotel was up the street across from the Beefsteak House. Dave picked up his horse at the eatery and took her to the livery barn. He dismounted and led the gray into the stall she had been using, stripped the saddle and blanket, and put some oats in the feed box. He yelled three times before the night man came out of the little office.

"Give my gray some more oats when she

cleans that up. Jackson is the moniker, isn't it?"

The man nodded.

"You don't talk too much."

"I save my talk for my friends," Jackson said.

Dave smiled. "I hope you don't get too lonely around here then." He turned and went quickly toward the hotel.

A half hour later Dave was washing the grime of the trail off his face at the basin in Room 12, second floor back. He had asked for this room especially, and made obvious preparations for bed. After he turned the lamp out he opened the window wide and rolled up three extra blankets and stuffed them under the blankets. The bundle looked like a sleeping man. Dave leaned a chair against the wall six feet from the window and waited.

Slade Jackson. He thought of the man most of the time. His voice was low and smooth all right. Was he really the one who had murdered his father? He would find out.

Dave nodded and almost dozed off once, but fear kept him awake, because if he were correct there was the threat of a club or a knife or a muffled forty-four awaiting those rolled-up blankets tonight.

It had been after midnight by the big clock in the lobby when Dave climbed the stairs. It was at least an hour after he turned out the light before he heard the scrapings on the flat roof outside his window. This was the easiest room in the hotel to get in or out of since the roof was almost flat here and a short drop to the ground. This was why he had chosen the room.

Dave lowered the chair to the floor and crouched next to the wall, listening to the slow progress of the person outside. At last a hand reached through the window, then another and a form cautiously levered inside the window and stood on the floor. The man tensed, then looked at the bed and moved purposefully toward it. A knife flashed up and down.

Dave stood and cocked his six-gun.

"Hold it right there! Turn around slowly."

The intruder stood, knife raised, then turned and threw the blade at Dave. Dave had dropped to one knee as he saw the man move and then he fired. Dave heard a groan as the man was knocked back onto the bed by the force of the forty-four slug.

The man did not move. Dave took the lamp from the near wall, lighted it and held it high. His forty-four was cocked and ready in the other hand as he moved up to the bed. The form lay on its back, one hand thrown over the face, a dark red stain soaking the right shoulder of a good black broadcloth suit. Dave pushed the hand away from the face as the man began to stir.

"Josh Mankin!" Dave said out loud, and put down the lamp. He shook the lawyer. Gradually booze-bleary eyes blinked and his head nodded and finally the eyes held on Dave.

"Dave, what you doing here? I came to kill a rat. To kill the rat who killed my Janie!"

"What was it? Who killed her?"

"Told me he was in Room 12. Helped me up here. They said the man in here killed my Janie."

Dave jumped back from some sixth sense he was hardly aware of. Two shots blasted into the room from the open window.

# CHAPTER EIGHT

One shot rammed a bullet into the white shirt front of Josh Mankin where his left pocket was. Josh was dead before the echo of the shots had stilled. The second shot had been meant for Dave, but missed when Dave moved and instead shattered the water pitcher on the table near the door.

Dave rolled toward the window and edged his head up in time to see two men leaping off the roof to the alley below. He didn't have time to fire a shot at them, and they would be lost in the jumble of buildings before he could get downstairs.

It took almost an hour to get Doc Bevins over to the hotel to certify Josh's death and have the body carried out. By that time Dave wasn't sleepy anymore. He'd set a trap, but had killed one of the men who might have helped him.

After Dave told Sheriff Zedicher the story, the lawman shook his head. "If Josh had given you the names of his helpers, I could have had your killer in ten minutes."

"My trap worked," Dave said. "But I caught the wrong man. Next time I'll get the killer."

The sheriff took the body down to the jail. Since there was no undertaker in town the job fell to the sheriff to see that burial was quick and efficient.

Dave raised one hand at Doc Bevins before he left the hotel and the small man remained behind. "I'm checking out. You got a cot I could catch a couple of winks on?"

"Yep. This place don't seem none too healthy."

Five minutes later when the door to Doc Bevins' house-office was safely bolted, Dave dropped his saddlebags and asked the question that had been nagging at him.

"How is Old Charley? Did he make it?"

"He'll live. I don't know why. Wheezing almost stopped and he has strong times when he's rational as you or me."

"Can he talk?"

The balding head shook. "He tries, but it's grunts and moans and rasping sounds. Can't make sense of it. Maybe in a week or two." He looked at Dave's face. "A mule's been walking on your face. Sit down."

Doc Bevins began checking the banged-up face as Dave talked. He covered everything that had happened since late the night before.

"Doc, you said last time I was here that

the whole valley was tensed up about something. What is it?"

Doc Bevins applied a new court plaster to the deepest cut on Dave's forehead as he talked. "It was about six months ago, now," the doctor said, "that this English guy came into town. All veddy proper and with his stuffy English accent. Said he was looking for good cattle land to buy. Stopped at the bank and they certified his assets — more than a hundred thousand dollars in a St. Louis bank. Then he rode around looking at ranches.

"His story was that he wanted to get a concentrated range area he could fence off like they did in England and raise cattle.

"The whole town was steamed up over it. And he was paying ten per cent more than anyone ever offered around here. Right away the big talk starts. Gold in Broken River! Silver in the mountains!

"Most of the ranchers, including your pa, were leery about selling. Some just didn't want to sell at any price. In the end, the English guy packed up and headed for Montana. Said something about it being closer to the prime markets.

"Now we haven't seen the swish of his moustache around here for two or three months."

"Did it look like a land grab to you, Doc?"

The bald head shook. "Nope. Just this rich bird trying to go into ranching in a big way."

"Is there any tie-in between him and Contway grabbing those two ranches on the Broken River and trying for the Circle K?"

"I don't know, Dave. But somehow it's got to be connected: him, Contway and your pa's bushwhacking."

Dave folded out a blanket on the floor. "It's too late to talk sense tonight. See you in the morning." Dave stretched out and was asleep before the medical man could turn down the lamp.

The next morning Dave had the kitchen range fire burning brightly when Doc Bevins came downstairs. Dave ate four eggs and a big chunk of bread painted with butter. They continued the conversation of the night before.

"Doc, what about Janie? Who would want to kill her? I've seen some dirty killing outlaws, but not even the worst of them would shoot a woman, let alone kill one with his hands. Does it take a special kind of man to do this? And could I pick that kind out?"

Doc Bevins shook his head. "I had one

course in medical insanity and the teacher didn't even know what he was talking about. That was a long time ago. Crazy? Sure men go crazy, kill crazy. And I guess some of them could go woman-kill crazy. Pick him out? Not me. Maybe in a hundred years we'll know more about insanity and what makes people do things. Not now."

"Would a man who could do this act like he hated all women, all the time?"

"Could be."

"Thanks, Doc," Dave said, feeling better after a few hours of sleep. He had three jobs to do and he outlined them to the medical man.

"First I'll file with the sheriff about contesting that bill of sale. Then I want to talk with the bank, and I'm going to try to put Josh's law case records in a good safe place until we get this all cleared up."

Doc Bevins frowned.

"What's the matter, Doc?"

"You! You eat like a young stallion. You'd better bring me a couple of dozen eggs from the General Store next time you stop in!"

Dave swung his hat at the old doctor's balding head and stood up. "Time for me to move. If you hear anything around town about my problem, you let me know." He went through the office and outside.

It was less than a block to the sheriff's office, and Dave was covering the distance in long, sure strides, his forty-four tied down carefully midway on his leg where he liked it. He had just passed the General Store when somebody called to him from the alley.

He looked in the alley, but couldn't see anyone. He thought he saw a slight movement behind some crates twenty yards ahead. Dave took out the forty-four and went into the narrow area carefully, checking both sides as he moved, hugging the side of the building to make a small target.

The gun muzzle that jammed into his side was a total surprise. Someone had followed him.

"Well, well, if it ain't the gent-ul-man from St. Lou," said a voice from behind him that Dave immediately knew was Hank Contway's. "Welcome home, drifter! Just walk ahead nice and careful like, cause I got mighty tender trigger fingers. That's right, on down there a ways more. We got ourselves something to settle."

Dave had been walking slowly. Now he turned and looked at Contway, then ahead where two men had idled into the alley — the Larchmont brothers. Midway in the long alley Contway stopped the procession.

Dave saw the Contway guns in one direction, and the two Larchmont guns the other way.

"Contway the killer," Dave said snorting. "You let those two idiots blast away at me from up there and you'll be catching as much of their lead as I will."

Contway nodded. "You got a point, drifter. Back up against that wall, easy like!" Dave moved back a step or two toward the wall and a heavy wooden packing crate that lay there. Contway circled him, gun trained on Dave all the time.

"You really as fast as you think, Contway?"

"I'm faster, Kemp."

"Then try me. Put that gun back in your holster and try me. You got two more guns backing your play."

Contway hesitated.

Dave pressed his momentary advantage.

"Scared, Contway? Afraid I might be as fast as you? Hear that, Larchmonts? Your big gunslinger boss here is afraid to match me!"

It worked. Contway said something over his shoulder, and the brothers, now ten yards behind him, eased their six-guns into the open as Contway holstered his.

"Any time you're ready, big-mouth drifter." Contway spat.

Dave relaxed his whole body, then in a surge of action dove to his left toward the wall and the heavy wooden packing crate. He drew his forty-four as he hit the ground and held it to his stomach as he rolled. He heard two shots, but the lead missed.

Then Dave was firing himself, smashing a slug into the shoulder of Contway and snapping another shot at the first man he saw as Contway spun backwards.

It was all over in six seconds. Contway sat in the dusty alley holding his shoulder. One Larchmont was on the ground, the other dropped his six-gun and stood with his hands in the air.

Dave came from behind the box slowly, and relaxed as he saw Contway's weapon in the dust.

"Get him, Curley! Get him, Bill! Gun him down!" Contway yelled.

"Not me, Hank," Curley said. "Not Bill either — I think he's dead."

Contway looked at his gunman. The bullet had caught Bill Larchmont just below the chin and had almost taken his head off.

Dave looked at the blood-splattered head and rode down an impulse to vomit. He had never killed a man before, and it wasn't as simple as it looked. He felt sweat forming over his eyes as he watched

Contway. The little man turned, holding his right shoulder, and yelled again at Curley. Dave noticed Contway's left gun was still holstered.

"Curley, go get the sheriff. Tell him Kemp just bushwhacked us and killed Bill. Said he was getting even with us for messing him yesterday. Move, Curley!"

"Stay put, Curley," Dave said quietly. He still held his six-gun and Curley nodded.

"Go, Curley. Make a run for it!" Contway bellowed. Curley didn't move. Contway sagged a little. He winced as he moved his right arm to a more comfortable position. Then looked at Kemp.

"You going to let me bleed to death, Kemp?"

"It's a good idea," Dave said. His mouth still tasted of the bile that had surged up. Dave reached to help Contway get to his feet. The wounded man leaned heavily against Dave and staggered, and Dave's gun hand came up to support the man.

Suddenly Contway turned and slammed his left fist down on Kemp's right hand and the sixgun fell into the dirt. Contway drew his left-hand Colt and stood back sneering.

"Never give a sucker an even break, Kemp, remember that. I learned it the hard way getting slickered out of a gold mine." He turned to Curley who hadn't moved. "Now get out of here and bring the sheriff, you gutless longhorn!" Curley ran out the near end of the alley.

Dave looked at his gun in the dirt, then at Contway.

"I shore hope you try for it, drifter. I'll put five holes clean through you!" Contway said as he saw the direction of Kemp's glance.

Dave looked up at Contway, and his eye caught a movement in the alley behind the gunman. Just a flash disappearing behind a door. Any witness at this point would help, Dave decided.

"Why did you send for the sheriff, Contway? You know that was a fair fight. You drew and fired before I did, and so did Bill back there. But you both missed and my lead hit. What can you prove?"

Contway laughed. "Prove? I don't have to prove nothing. Curley says what I tell him to, and we both say you bushwhacked the three of us for beating you up. That eye of yours open yet?"

"I shot in self-defense. How you going to prove otherwise?"

"I don't have to prove it, Kemp. Because you ain't gonna be around to tell the judge nothing." Contway raised the six-gun from his side and centered it on Dave's chest.

# CHAPTER NINE

They were only standing four feet apart.
Contway couldn't miss at this range, Dave
thought.

"You tried to run, I had to shoot! Easy,
huh?" Contway smiled at his own cleverness.

"So you shot me in the chest when I was
running away?" Dave asked, stalling. He
had to figure something. Then he remembered the movement back in the alley. It
might have been a man.

"Turn around, Kemp."

"So you can shoot me in the back like
you did my pa?"

"I never shot your pa."

"Then you know who did!"

"Shut up, Kemp, and turn around."

Dave ignored him. He took his black hat
off and began swatting himself with it,
slapping off the alley dust. Suddenly he
slammed the hat into Contway's face.

Instantly Dave dove at Contway's legs
and felt the hot flash of the muzzle blast of
the forty-five as it roared over his head.
Then he hit Contway and sent him

smashing to the ground against his right shoulder and Contway dropped the revolver and twisted his face in pain. Dave drove his fist stiffly into Contway's jaw and the fight was over. He picked up his own gun and both of Contway's and stared down at the man whining in the dust.

Dave looked up as a form came out of the doorway down the alley. It was Sheriff Zedicher.

Contway saw him too.

"Sheriff, lock up Kemp! He just shot down Bill Larchmont in cold blood. Bill didn't even have his gun out!"

"Shut up, Contway. I heard the whole thing from the alley. Now get out of here, and take that ex-gunswift with you. The county ain't gonna bury him."

"But Sheriff!"

"Ride out, cowboy!"

"I want my guns first."

Dave shrugged when the lawman looked at him. He broke open each revolver and spilled the shells into the dust, then tossed the guns to Contway.

They watched the shorter man walk stiffly toward Main Street, his right arm held carefully at his side.

Dave picked up his hat and slapped the rest of the alley dust off his pants.

"If you're headed back for your office, Sheriff, I'd like to fill in that complaint."

The sheriff nodded. "Nothing more doing here."

It took only five minutes for Dave to work out the legal paper and get the sheriff to sign it. Then he left. He wasn't ready to tell the lawman what Sue had heard. He didn't want to get her involved. Now that he had seen her again, he didn't want her hurt in any way — even if it slowed down his hunt.

Dave went into the bank next and signed the deposit forms to take over the savings account. When he was through he looked up at Lyle Archer. The banker wore a touch of sadness in his eyes.

"I'm sorry about all this, Dave," Archer said. "If there's ever anything I can do . . ." He stood up.

"How is Sue, Mr. Archer?"

"Sue? Oh, she's . . . fine." He paused. "No, no she isn't. Last two weeks she's been flighty and nervous. Like she was scared of her own shadow. We can't figure it out." He blinked and smiled. "But you have your own troubles. Remember, now, Dave, anything I can do, just call."

Dave stood and smiled. It was good to

have a banker on your side. He said goodbye and headed for the courthouse. He had to file his complaint contesting the sale of the property, and he was curious about the land records. A good look over the homesteading and open-range map might give him some clues.

The courthouse was a small building set halfway down the block from the bank. It was a temporary location until money could be found to build a stone courthouse on the square block of land Lyle Archer had given to the county. Dave found the clerk and gave him the dollar for the filing fee.

"Chance I can look at your land map?"

The clerk eyed him a moment, then nodded. "Guess it's all right since you're a property owner. The roll-down map back there marked 'C' is the one."

Dave grinned at the clerk's self-importance. The maps were public records and anyone could see them. The map on the north end of the county was about the same as Dave remembered. There were six or seven ranches that had been homesteaded originally in the bottom land where the grass grew. Seven or eight ranches clustered around Lewis River and the middle fork and Broken River's main fork. But there was no pattern. The three ranches that

Hank Contway had or tried to get were all on the main fork. Was someone trying to tie up the water supply for the whole valley? But who? Contway? Somehow Dave still couldn't believe it. Contway simply wasn't a planner. He lived too much for today to have long-range plans.

He stepped back and took a longer look at the area. There had to be an answer here somewhere, a better one than water rights. But where was it? Dave went back to the clerk.

"That English fella here a few months back. Did he actually buy any land?" Dave asked.

The clerk shook his head. "Only time we saw him was when he looked at those maps."

Dave thanked the clerk and left, slanting across the street to the office Josh Mankin had used for his law practice. Dave had cleared with the sheriff earlier that morning. Josh had no relatives in the area, so Dave asked if he could lock up the files and records until he could buy them and take over the practice. The lawman said that would be fair and had forced the door lock.

Dave spent an hour and a half boxing the files and taking them to the courthouse for storage. It was the safest place in town besides the jail. When the task was done,

Dave stopped at the Golden Girl and ordered a beer. The place had just opened for the day, and only one card game was being played at the back tables. None of the girls was around. Dave called the bartender.

"Elly still work here?" he asked when the bartender turned.

"Sure, and she'll still be here after we're both gone," the barman said. He nodded at the door behind the bar. "She's in there jawboning the boss about something."

Dave laughed. "That sounds like the same old Elly. Tell her Dave Kemp is out here."

The barkeep grinned and delivered the message. A few minutes later the door behind the bar opened and a woman edged through it. She was larger than Dave remembered, well over three hundred and seventy-five pounds now.

"Daveee! I remember the night you had your first beer! That was a night!"

She had changed little in two years, Dave decided. The rouge was a little thicker, the henna-red hair a little coarser, folds of pink flesh a little paler than they had been, and you still couldn't tell where her huge breasts stopped and her bulging stomach started. But her face was pert and dainty, and Dave marveled how it could

stay so normal while the rest of her bal-
looned. Her blue eyes snapped and her
thin lips curved into a lecherous smile.

"You want me to fix you up with some
morning action, Daveee?"

"Afraid not, Elly. Got a problem. You
heard about my pa?"

She nodded, her smile gone.

"Did you hear about my sister, Janie?"

Tears brimmed from Elly's eyes, then
splashed down over red cheeks. She didn't
try to stop them or dab them away.

"I'm looking for a killer, Elly. Anything
you can tell me?"

"Davee, we can't repeat . . ."

"This isn't just backyard gossip, Elly!"

She stopped crying and blew her nose
noisily. "For you we can try, Davee. I'll ask
around. No promises."

Dave nodded. "Good. Now, Elly, what
type of a man does it take to kill a woman?"

Elly stared at the back of the booth, and
Dave wasn't sure she had heard him. Then
her face blanched and her eyes glazed, her
voice became almost a whisper.

"I thought I'd forgotten," she said. "I
saw it happen once — on the river boat.
He was just a man, not much different
from the others. But he killed her. He said
she was no good, just like his wife, and he

killed her. With his hands around her throat!" Elly lowered her head onto her huge arms for a moment. When she looked up she had come back from the nightmare and she looked at him coldly.

"He was a madman, they said. They hung him."

"Elly, is a man like that different? In here, for instance, have you ever seen anyone who acted like he did, even just for a minute?"

One thick-fingered hand rubbed her forehead, then she shook her head. "No, Dave. Some of the cowboys get mean drunk, but that's not the same. It's the way this one looked, his eyes. No, I ain't seen nobody with eyes like that since I left the boat that night."

"Watch for him, Elly. He's here some-where, the killer, and I aim to find him!"

Dave stood quickly, walked out through the Golden Girl batwings, and continued along the wooden sidewalks in front of the stores. He wished he had ridden down here. It was more than a block to the livery stable. He lifted his hat and resettled it. At least he was back in the cowboy mold. Any good puncher worth his saddle would never walk ten feet if he could saddle his bronc and ride there. The feeling soon melted away and another took its place. He needed to see Sue again. She might have thought of something else she hadn't told him last night.

He wanted to check her story again. At last he quit arguing with himself. Okay, so he just wanted to see her again. What he thought had died so long ago must not have perished completely.

Dave saddled his horse at the livery stable, wishing he had a saddle equipped the way the sheriff did for long distance riding. He would have to fix his later. Dave mounted and kicked the gray into motion toward the Archer house.

The sun was two hours from noon when he dropped off the horse and walked past the picket-fence gate and to the Archer front door. Mrs. Archer answered his knock.

"Good morning, David," she said with a smile. "Nice to have you home again. I missed seeing you last night."

"Thanks, ma'am. Sure good to be back. Is Sue here?"

"No, David. She left over an hour ago. A boy brought a note from Mrs. Hanson saying she was ill and asking Susan to come out for a day or two. She is a favorite of Mrs. Hanson, you know."

"Yes, ma'am." He paused. "Guess I'll

see her later. Thanks."

The Hanson place was not far out of his way back to the ranch. He should ride to the Circle K, anyway, and check to see how the new crew was coming along. He looked at his saddlebags. This would be a good time to get them packed with some jerky and beans and crackers that he could use on the trail. He mounted and rode for the General Store.

Ten minutes later Dave had his purchases lashed down on his saddle. He had emergency food, a blanket roll and some extra stinkers wrapped in an oiled paper. It all packed neatly into the saddlebags or tied on.

Dave turned his horse toward Middle Fork Road and headed out of town. The Hanson place was just half a mile away near a little bend in the river. They had a garden irrigated from a small canal, and a cow and a few chickens, and a host of friends. It was like Mrs. Hanson to call on Sue when she needed help. Before long someone would have to care for them. Neither had any family living here.

Dave wondered about not seeing a carriage at the house when he came up. He tied his mount to a tree and Blaine Hanson came outside to meet him. Blaine was in his seventies, and you could see the effects of the hard life of a dirt-farmer. His hands were gnarled and twisted, and his face was lean and weathered.

"Dave Kemp! Ain't seen you in more'n two year. Back East I hear," the old farmer said.

"Right," Dave said, taking the man's hand in greeting. He paused. "Is Sue Archer here?"

"Susie? Why, nope. She ain't been out in two, three weeks."

Dave tensed, remembering. A boy brought a note, Mrs. Archer had said. He looked at Mr. Hanson. "Your wife sick?"

"Land sakes no! This is canning day. A woman can't be sick on canning day!"

Dave's hand rubbed the smooth leather on his holster. "Did you send a note to Sue?"

"No we didn't, boy. Something wrong?"

"It might be, Mr. Hanson!" Dave ran back to his horse, mounted and rode for town. Only a few minutes later he reined in at the livery stable. The same man Dave had seen before, the day stable man, ambled out.

"Slade Jackson around?" Dave asked.

"He works nights."

"He around now?"

"Nope."

"Know where he is?"

"Nope."

Dave slid off the gray and moved toward the other man quickly.

"Now what you doing?" the stable man said. "You leave me alone!"

Dave grabbed the blue cotton shirt front and twisted. "You tell me what I want to know and I won't hurt you."

The head nodded.

"Is Slade Jackson here?"

"No."

"Where'd he go?"

"Said he was going to Saddle Mountain South to shoot a deer."

"When did he leave?"

"About three hours ago. He took two horses. Said he needed one to pack out the deer. Took his rifle, and headed toward Middle Fork Road."

"Saddle Mountain is in the other direction. Why did he go out Middle Fork?"

"I don't know."

Dave's hand relaxed on the cloth and the man rubbed his throat. "Why you pushin' so hard?" the stable man asked.

"Never mind." Dave ran for his horse and swung up. Middle Fork Road went past the Hansons' house. He kept the gray at a slow trot through town, then let her out as he passed the last house for the half mile run to the Hansons'. This time he noticed the fresh buggy tracks, but they went right on past the little house. On a hunch he followed them, and a quarter of a mile farther on they turned into an abandoned ranch. The buggy was hidden behind some trees, and the one horse was loosely tied to some brush. This must have been Sue's rig.

He backtracked down the road a hundred yards, then swung out into the prairie on the mountain side of the road. He made a quick study of the familiar landmarks.

To reach Saddle Mountain South, Jackson would have to move southeast from town. But if he had planned to kidnap the girl, why had he left so many signs, and even told the day stable man where he was headed? It could be a trap, Dave knew, but a trap with undeniable bait. Even if it were a trap, he had to walk into it. He had to find Sue!

Then he remembered the strange un-smiling eyes of Slade Jackson. What was it Elly had said? It was the *look* in a madman's eyes. Dave thought of his sister lying on her bed, and a jagged shiver flashed down his spine. He had to find Sue before it was too late!

# CHAPTER TEN

Dave rode hard for a quarter of a mile east into the prairie, then turned and headed south. He let the gray walk and leaned out of the saddle. He had to find hoofprints of a pair of horses heading southeast. He paced through the sage and the soft grass that had sprung up after the last rain, moving half a mile south, then turned east for another quarter mile, then moved north again trying to cut the trail. He was almost back to the north point when he found the sign he had been watching for. It showed two horses, moving fast, but not headed southeast — they were going almost straight east, toward Twin Sisters Peaks.

Dave stopped and looked at the sky. The sun was dead above him, burning through a slight haze. The day would be warm, and he had seven hours left for tracking. He stood high in the stirrups and looked east, but could see no sign of movement on the plain that stretched out to the foothills, which were now almost lost in the haze.

Dave slouched in the saddle as he rode,

watching the trail only occasionally, losing it momentarily, but finding it with a small "S" maneuver.

Then he gambled, kicked his mount into a gallop and moved almost a mile toward the foothills. The trail had arrowed directly to the valley that led up Mercer Creek, and Dave was sure now that was where the tracks were going. After the run, he let the horse blow for a moment, then moved in another gentle "S" curve until he cut the trail again. It was still glued in a rifle shot toward Mercer Creek canyon. Dave rode hard again, and covered three miles this time before he pulled up and walked as he looked for the trail. He found it quickly and noted that the marks of the hooves were not as deep now — the loaded horses were walking. He was gaining on them, but just how much he didn't know. Once the riders entered the timbered area of Mercer Creek, climbing toward the Sisters, they wouldn't be able to check the back trail, so there was a good chance Slade Jackson didn't know anyone was coming.

Dave pushed on, hitting Mercer Creek while there were still four hours of sunlight left. He watered the gray and let her rest. As she did he broke off a chunk of jerky for his jaw, stuffing more into his jacket pocket. Dave went upstream a few yards and drank. He refilled his canteen, then mounted and continued his tracking. The sign was where he knew it would be, on the old trapper's trail on the north side of the creek.

The two horses had moved in single file here, and the trail was easy to follow, but slow, since the path was old, and seldom used now. Often he had to detour around fallen trees and washouts.

Darkness dropped suddenly over the mountain the way the lights went out at the St. Louis opera house, and Dave hurriedly found a level spot where he could stretch out his blanket roll and tie his horse.

The heat of the day dissolved with the light and when the stars appeared, the cool night air stabbed through Dave's shirt and jacket. He huddled in the clearing and thought about building a lean-to, then shrugged. He was soft! He cut a few branches from a pine for a mattress, then wrapped himself in the blanket. He wanted to make a fire, but he knew how far the smell of smoke could travel in the clear mountain air. He couldn't risk warning those ahead so quickly that he was on the trail. It was his only advantage, and he had to hold it. As he slept the forty-four nestled close to his hand.

Dave awoke once, hearing a crashing in the brush far to his left, and decided some she-bear was out for a midnight snack. He was cold and numb and stiff, but rolled over on the pine and slept again. The east was a smudge of white when he woke up the second time. Jerky and a small can of beans were breakfast, then he climbed into the saddle, sore and aching in every cold joint. He moved out with the first light. The going was slower than he had expected and it took him another hour before he saw the clearing open ahead. He was near the top of the first slope, and a trapper had built a cabin here probably fifty years ago. Dave wished he could see better. His left eye was about half open now, but it still bothered him.

He slipped to the ground, tied his horse and moved to the edge of the woods, Indian-like. He went halfway around the clearing before he crawled up to the cabin. It had fallen in, but there was one corner where he found evidences of a bedroll, and under a board there was a small white handkerchief with an embroidered "S" in the corner. They must have stayed here last night, and pushed on to another place, he decided. He rode again.

The trail led to the top of the pass between the Sisters, and turned north for a quarter of a mile. The clearing here was larger, a natural glen with a small lake and a sturdy cabin that had been carefully built of foot-thick logs.

Dave approached the clearing a step at a time, using the trees for concealment and crawling the last few yards. He smelled the smoke before he saw it. A thin white-blue spire lifted easily in the windless, morning sky. There was no other sign.

He crawled back into the deeper cover of the trees and circled a quarter of the way around the building, then edged up for another look. Again there was no window, no door. He repeated the slow process and came up on the front side of the cabin, peering from behind a young pine tree. The cabin had one window, a foot square, high up, and a stout door which was shut tightly. The smoke rose at the same peaceful slowness. To the left, near the small lake, one horse grazed, untied on the new grass.

He settled to wait, and after an hour of no activity inside or outside the cabin, Dave crinkled his forehead. What was going on? Was there anyone inside? Was it really a trap? Either way, it was time he made his move.

Dave worked back the way he had come until he was hidden in the trees behind the cabin. Then he walked quickly to the side of the clearing and ran low and fast toward the back corner of the building. He paused and listened, but heard nothing.

Cautiously he edged his way along the wall to the corner, checked around it, then moved along the shorter wall to the front. The door now was only a foot away around the corner. He knew if Jackson was watching, he would be concentrating on the front of the cabin. With the rifle he would have time for one clean shot. Dave reached around the corner, keeping his arm low to the ground, and tried to push the door open. It wouldn't move.

Dave reached behind him, picked up a stick he had seen, and pushed it up toward the thumb-piece latch. The stick wavered, then came down on the latch and the door eased open. Dave caught it and pulled it open a foot, then wiggled around the corner logs and was halfway inside the door when a rifle slug slammed into the door. Before the gunman could fire again, Dave crawled inside the cabin and pulled the door shut.

He paused, listening, but there were no more shots. He bolted the door from his side and looked into the gloom. There was a muffled moan, and when his eyes began working in the dim light, he saw a figure on a bunk in the corner. It was Sue Archer, and as he rushed over he saw there was a gag in her mouth and that her hands were tied with rawhide and lashed to the bunk post.

He took the gag out of her mouth tenderly and nestled her brown-haired head against his chest as he cut the rawhide away from the post. She was sobbing as he helped her stand. Then he held her in his arms and tried to quiet her crying.

"Sue, it's all right. Sue, I'm here, and he can't hurt you now."

He held her tightly then and heard her sobbing die out to a short sniffle and finally her hand came up to wipe away the tears.

"Dave! Oh, Dave! I knew you'd come!" Her tear-stained eyes were filled with joy and relief, but too quickly her happiness turned to fear. "But he said you'd come up and then he'd take care of you when you did! He left this morning and now . . . he'll kill you, and then me, and oh! I wish you never had come!"

She was crying again, quietly this time, in desperation. Dave kissed her on the forehead and shook her gently. "Now look, Sue Archer. We're not dead yet. And I don't intend to be. It is Slade Jackson we're talking about, isn't it?"

She nodded.

A rock smashed through the one pane of glass in the high window and Sue shivered in his arms. Dave held her as the voice stabbed into the room.

"Glad you finally got here, Kemp. Been waiting. Sneaky the way you got inside, but it don't matter."

Dave held his finger to his lips for silence and they listened, but could hear only the wind whispering through the pine branches high above.

"Don't play no games with me, Kemp. I know you're in there. You come out nice and peaceful and you can die like a man. Stay in there and I'll burn you out! You got three minutes to decide!"

"Dave, what can we do?" Sue whispered. "He means it. He'll kill us without even thinking about it. He, he hurt me last night. He made me tell him what I heard at the livery stable."

Dave's frown hardened. "He hurt you?"

"I'm all right." She held out her right wrist. "He grabbed me here and twisted until I screamed. And then I told him. I'm not very brave."

"He'll pay for that, Sue!" Dave looked

around the cabin. It was as solid as a pine log. He pushed aside a small rug on one end of the earth-packed floor. There was no cellar, no tunnel. The window was too high for any use. They were blind. Trapped in a log cabin with a crazy man outside with guns.

Dave looked at the window. It might work. He pushed a small table to the front wall and stood up on it. He raised his head quickly and looked out the broken window, then jerked his head down. A pistol slug rammed through the remaining window glass, and Dave jumped down, unhurt.

"He's about thirty feet in front of the cabin," Dave said. "He's behind a log and the stump out there, and his saddlebag is close by." Dave took out his six-gun and checked the loads. "Better lay on the bunk and keep your head down," he cautioned Sue.

Dave went to the door and eased the inside bolt back quietly. Then in the same motion he pushed the door open a foot, leaned around it and snapped three quick shots at the log and stump, then closed the door and threw the bolt.

No answering shots or sounds came from outside, only the high murmur of the pines. Then Dave heard a bolt slide into place on the outside of the door.

"Now, Kemp, you won't be throwing no more lead at me. Your time is up. Toss your six-gun out the window!"

"Come in and get us, Slade," Dave called. "A fair fight should be a novelty for you!"

"You're a dead man, Kemp!"

Sue Ann moved close to him and he slipped his arm around her shoulders. "Don't worry," Dave whispered. "I'll get us out of this." But he didn't have the slightest idea how.

They heard the crackle of the fire very quickly, and smelled the smoke. Dry pine boughs must have been used, Dave thought. Smoke began seeping in under the door.

"Sit down, Sue," Dave said as the smoke kept coming. They sat on the bunk, then on the floor. Soon the door was hot to the touch. Dave went over it again. He could see no way out.

Jackson's voice came over the sound of the fire.

"Just throw that six-gun out the window, Kemp, and I'll put out the fire."

Dave felt his gunbelt. He hadn't reloaded since those three shots. He took one of the forty-four bullets and looked at it. Powder!

If he could get the rounds apart he could use the powder to make a small bomb! The fireplace had a set of rusted fire tongs. They might work!

His eyes were smarting now. "Sue, take the cartridges out of my gunbelt." He worked quickly. With the tongs he held the metal shell casing, and with his teeth he slowly twisted on the lead slug. Dave thought his jaw would come unhinged before the first of the lead slugs began to twist. Then he had it off and looked for a container. A small can or a bottle. He saw a tobacco sack. Perfect! He had twelve of the shells emptied when he called to Jackson.

"You win, Jackson. I'm throwing out my six-gun."

Dave worked quickly while Sue made two tries to throw the unloaded weapon out the hole. Then Dave took it and jumped up and pushed it through.

He went back to work with the shells, stuffing the empty casings and lead slugs into his pocket so Jackson wouldn't find them. The smoke was getting worse. Sue Ann lay close to the floor now and Dave noticed the smoke at the door diminish. Jackson was putting out the fire.

Dave had four more shells to unload

when Jackson slammed open the bolt on his side of the door.

"Open the door, smart guy," Jackson said. "You come out first, Kemp!"

Dave pulled the string on the tobacco sack, less than half full of black powder — but it would have to do. Now if he could get a chance to use it! He shoved it into his coat pocket and motioned to Sue Ann to come with him as he went to the door.

"Do exactly what he tells you, and don't worry!" He turned to the door. "I'm coming out, Jackson." Dave threw the bolt open and pushed the door. The light blinded him as he staggered over the remains of the fire and into the sunshine.

The first thing Dave could focus on were the slate-gray eyes of Slade Jackson and the six-gun aimed at Dave's chest. Then at the last moment the muzzle shifted and the blue-orange flame leaped at him and the lead ripped into his upper arm like a sledgehammer, spinning him around and throwing him back against the cabin wall.

Dave grabbed his arm. Blood seeped through his fingers and he felt his eyes start to glaze, but he fought back to consciousness. "Not now!" "Stand up!" "Where's Sue?" His mind rifled commands and he obeyed. At least his arm would move. The slug had missed the bone. He held the arm tightly as his eyes cleared.

Slade Jackson was laughing in front of him. Then Sue Ann was there beside him. She lifted her skirt and tore a long strip of cloth from her petticoat. Then she gently removed his fingers from the arm and wrapped the band of white cloth around the gash tightly, stopping the flow of blood. Dave looked at the wound as she worked. It was a deep gash across his arm, painful but not disabling.

Jackson shook his head and pointed at Dave. "The look on your face when you knew I was going to shoot! You looked dead already!" He stopped laughing. "Just the first payment, Kemp. Just the first!" He looked at Sue. "Don't make that too good. He don't need that arm. He won't need no arms at all this time tomorrow!"

Jackson peered at them again, nodding his head. "Hey, you! Come here!"

Dave barely nodded and Sue went toward Jackson. She stopped in front of him out of reach.

"You like this woman, Kemp? Like her lots, I hear."

"Jackson, you're crazy. You're sick in the head! An animal!"

The shot surprised Dave, who never saw

Jackson's draw. The bullet thudded into the log wall a foot from Dave's hip.

"Stop calling me names! I'll shoot your legs out from under you. I'll carve on this female and make you watch! Or maybe just toss you on the rest of that bonfire!"

Dave looked and saw the remains of the pine bough fire burning near the front door. The fire would work nicely to explode the bomb if he could get Jackson near it.

Jackson had stepped up to Sue now. He looked at her coldly, then laughed. "Tell Dave 'bout the good time we had in that trapper cabin last night, woman!"

"We did not! We . . ."

Jackson slapped her with the back of his hand and Sue Ann dropped to her knees. Dave lunged from the wall, but the gun hand came up with iron and Dave stopped.

"Stay, Kemp! Good dog. Now stand up, woman! Stand up!"

Sue Ann struggled to her feet, her head bowed.

"Look at me, woman!" She looked up slowly and when her chin was held high again, Jackson grabbed the front of her dress and yanked down, savagely. The shoulder seams parted and the whole front of the garment ripped away and hung to her waist. The force of the attack pulled

Sue to her knees again. She frantically pulled the torn cloth over her shoulders and Dave looked away.

He hardly knew when he started moving. His aching arm was forgotten as he charged the ten feet toward Jackson. Better to die now, he thought, as he saw the blue steel of the six-gun come up. When he crashed into the man he felt no bullet, but the side of the gun slashed down on his head and he slipped away from Jackson and dropped to the ground. Dirt and leaves smothered his face and he remembered the shovels of earth he had thrown into Janie's grave. Then he knew only blackness.

# CHAPTER ELEVEN

The sun stood well past midday when Dave became aware he was still alive. He was lying on his stomach where he had fallen, his face still rooted into the soft dirt of the clearing and his bullet-furrowed arm throbbing and oozing blood. He became aware of all this slowly, but held himself rigid and unmoving until he was sure he was fully conscious. He opened one eye and looked around cautiously. No one was in sight. He lifted his head slightly and the pounding against his skull made him gasp. He looked toward the cabin. Sue Ann worked at a small cooking fire laid near the stump. Jackson sat on the stump cleaning his rifle.

Dave sat up and groaned. The bald-headed man came off the stump palming his Colt out of leather. Then he pushed it back and walked over to Dave.

"Lazy saddle tramp, sleeping in the middle of the day. You been snoring away for two hours," Jackson said.

Dave looked at Sue. Her dress was

covering her again. She must have pinned it together. He glared at Jackson, but the bald man snorted.

"Not yet, Kemp. I ain't touched her yet. I want you to watch! Now get over here!"

Dave stood slowly, agonizingly. The gash had only bled a little, but his head was a thousand swarming bees and his eyes kept blurring and coming back into focus. He moved painfully toward the fire. The fire was a good one. Sue Ann had a can on for coffee and half a rabbit on a spit. He shuffled toward the fire as Jackson stood on the other side.

Dave felt the bulge on his right-hand jacket pocket. The sack of powder was still there. Now if he could get Sue away from the fire.

"Water," he said softly. "Could I have some water?" He looked at Jackson.

"I'm not your slave, Kemp. Woman! Get some water!"

Sue Ann looked up, then went toward the pump. Dave turned to watch her, and when he turned back the sack of powder was in his hand. Jackson had squatted by the fire to get more coals around the coffee can. Dave tossed the sack into the fire in front of Jackson and stepped back.

The instant the sack hit the coals it

exploded. The explosion wasn't what Dave had expected, but there was an immediate heavy "poof" as the black powder burned quickly and showered sparks and coals and a heavy cloud of smoke into Jackson's face.

Dave surged forward, stepped over the fire and hit Jackson in the chest with his good shoulder while the other man dug at his eyes with his knuckles. Jackson went down with Dave on top of him. He kicked away the gun that Slade clawed for, and Sue ran and picked it up. Dave smashed his left fist into Jackson's face time after time and his brain kept saying more! more!

The roar of the forty-four jolted him back to reality and he saw Sue holding the smoking gun which pointed at the blue sky.

Ten minutes later Sue had done exactly as Dave told her and Slade Jackson was tied securely. It took them half an hour more to find the third horse, and to saddle all three. Dave could not move his right arm above his waist, so Sue made a sling for it from another strip of white petticoat.

"Untie his feet, Sue, so he can ride," Dave said when they were ready. Sue Ann did and brought his horse. She let Jackson mount, and held the reins. Dave struggled into his saddle and then Sue Ann swung up into the leather, astride, with her skirt flapping on both sides. Before the procession moved, Dave called to Jackson, "Watch."

Then Dave drew with his left hand and fired, spinning a tin can in the dust. "Remember, Jackson, I can shoot with my left hand, too!"

The prisoner glowered, and Dave knew death was never very far away when Slade Jackson was around.

Sue led the way, holding the reins of Jackson's horse, and Dave followed. He hoped to make it to the bottom of the forest trail before dark, so they could ride on into town through the prairie in the moonlight.

It was slow going. The pine and scrub oak seemed thicker and more tangled now than when they had ridden up. Dave's arm was pounding and his head ached with a perpetual numbing steadiness.

They stopped once to refill the canteens and chew on some jerky, then moved down the twisting trail toward the bottom of the mountain. They broke out of the tree cover with about two hours to dark. Jackson had offered no resistance, and this worried Dave. Slade was not a man to give up easily — when he knew a rope waited for him in town.

The shadows of the hills were well out ahead of them now as they began to move across the flatness of the valley floor, with only a twisting arroyo slanting off to the left. Dave began to relax a little when Sue's mount stepped into a gopher hole and shied suddenly to one side spilling Sue from the saddle. Jackson had been riding beside the girl with Dave just behind. Now the man turned and threw a handful of sand at the gray's head. The big horse reacted quickly to the stinging particles, lurched sideways and spun around. By the time Dave had her turned back, Jackson had kicked his horse into a full gallop and was headed for the gully which carried Mercer Creek.

Dave threw three quick shots toward the disappearing figure, then urged his gray forward. But eight or ten strides later Dave eased the big horse to a stop. His shoulder was on fire now, and each jolt stabbed it with hot needles. His head resounded with hammering like a smithy's anvil. He turned and went back to Sue Ann.

"Sorry, Dave. I'm making the mistakes. I haven't been thrown off a horse since I was seven," Sue said apologetically.

"My fault he got away, not yours. This head of mine is splitting wide open." Dave swung down and caught her horse and helped the girl mount. A white flash of knee showed through the skirts as she sat astride the horse. Sue Ann didn't seem to notice.

"I'd better get you into town to see Doc Bevins," she said.

They rode straight to the Archer house where there was a lot of crying from Mrs. Archer and Sue, and then Mrs. Archer had to kiss Dave twice.

"Wasn't till an hour ago we thought something might be wrong," Lyle Archer boomed. "Sue usually stays out at the Hansons' overnight. Then came dark tonight and we got worried."

Dave tried to leave quickly to go see Doc Bevins.

"Don't be foolish, Dave," Lyle said. "We'll get Doc Bevins over here in no time. Now sit down and let me get some booze into you!"

"I can go over there just as easy . . ."

"Won't hear of it. You brought Sue Ann back from that kidnapper, and got shot up and clubbed. It's the least I can do. Bet the sheriff can get a posse out after that Slade Jackson tomorrow morning. Shouldn't be too hard to find him. Unless he runs too far."

Dave shook his head. "Not tonight. We can't track him tonight." Dave took the glass the banker gave him and took a taste. Whiskey and branch water, mostly whiskey. He'd need it when Doc Bevins started jabbing around in his arm. He drank it, and then another, and was on his third when he saw the room begin to circle around him and turn into a blur. Soft, gentle hands guided him and lowered his head onto a pillow and then the softness melted into faded shades of blues and greens and then opaqueness.

He saw the knife coming but couldn't dodge it. It seemed to sink deep into his arm. Hands held him as the knife came at him again and this time he screamed.

He shook his head and blinked and the film slid away from his eyes. The hands were real — they were holding him down. And the scream was real — it was his own. The knife turned into a searing stream of turpentine that Doc Bevins was pouring into the bullet gash.

A gentle hand dabbed a handkerchief at the sweat on his brow and he saw Sue standing beside him in a clean dress. Her hair had been combed and she was biting her lip, trying to help him stand the pain.

"Easy, Doc!" Dave said.

The old doctor snorted. "Told you he was still alive. Too tough and mean to let one slug stop him."

The wound was soon cleaned and treated and bandaged. Doc Bevins stood up. "What's all this fuss about? Little old thing like that. Sting a little bit for a few days, but it won't stop you from working!"

It was almost an hour later before Dave could talk his way out of the house. Mrs. Archer had insisted that Dave stay right there in the guest room. Doc grinned and watched Dave squirm. When they had said goodbye and were outside, the old medic chuckled.

"Helen Archer almost had you hogtied there, boy."

"Almost is not a legal term, Doctor," Dave said, then sobered. "How is Old Charley?"

"Coming along. He's still alive, and I think he'll make it. He may never talk again, though."

The two horses stood tied at the fence. Dave swung up on his.

"You still ride a horse, Doc?"

"If I have to." He looked at the animal and then back at Dave. "This one I think

118

I'll lead. You in a hurry?"

Dave shook his head and they headed for the livery stable. They walked halfway to the stable when Doc Bevins turned and said, "If you plan on staying at my place you better bring a dozen eggs. Nearly ate me out of house and home last time."

"This time, Doc, I'll try the hotel. They got soft beds and I need one."

"Oh, my couch ain't good enough for you?"

"That's right, Doc. Why don't you get some decent furniture?"

"Why don't you pay your bill? I patched up your hide over an hour ago, and you ain't paid me yet."

Dave shook his head and laughed. "I'll argue the case with you later, you old coyote — when I've had a good night's sleep."

But Dave slept very little that night. The arm still burned like a branding iron and his headache was back, banging away like an anvil hammer. He finally got up and dressed just before daylight. The night clerk loaned him a razor and some hot water and Dave slashed off a two-day beard. He was at the Beefsteak House when it opened and put away a double order of steak and eggs and three cups of

119

coffee. He had discarded the sling Doc Bevins fixed for him, and found that by gritting his teeth only a little, he could let his right arm stretch out fully as he walked. Even his left eye was open now and working right for a change.

Dave headed for the sheriff's office. Before he had gone twenty feet a rangehand fell into stride with him.

"Hear Slade Jackson is running, that right, Dave?"

"Probably is. How you hear that?"

"All over town. Sheriff's forming up a posse right now."

As they came closer Dave could see a commotion in front of the jail. There were ten or twelve men on horses standing around, and more drifting in all the time.

The sheriff stood on the plank walk, waving at the men as they rode up. When he saw Dave he met him.

"You riding?" the sheriff asked.

"Of course," Dave said.

"Leave in ten minutes."

Dave turned and headed for the livery barn. When he had his gray saddled he looked at her closely. She was in no shape for another hard ride. He pulled off the leather and asked the livery man to bring him a horse from the corral. "Anything that would hold a saddle," Dave said.

The horse the man brought wasn't much, but Dave couldn't stop to argue. It was a paint, broad chested, but with a slightly wild look in its eye. Dave saddled up and trotted the pony back to the jail.

There were nearly thirty riders at the sheriff's office now. All were astride and ready for the trail.

"I'm swearing in all you men as Deputies of Lake County," the sheriff said. "Now remember, we want Jackson alive, no matter what he did."

Lyle Archer walked up stiffly, watching. "Sheriff, I'm giving a hundred dollar reward for Jackson, dead or alive! I want him brought back!"

"Can't stop you from offering, Lyle. But I'd lots rather make him stand trial for what he did to your niece." The sheriff turned. "Let's move out!" The sheriff mounted and headed out North Fork Road. He came up beside Dave.

"Now, show us where you lost Jackson," he said.

It was about an hour before the posse reached the spot where the bald-headed man had escaped. Dave showed the sheriff the tracks and the big man got down to look at them. Dave and two others stayed with the sheriff, who sent the body of the group to the side of the trail so it wouldn't be obliterated. Then the slow job of tracking began. Jackson moved north, then cut down a draw and headed back east, making no attempt to cover his trail. Then he went west and the trackers were shaking their heads. He was riding in patterns, yet apparently not trying to confuse his followers. They relaxed and when they did, the trail turned into a giant jigsaw puzzle. It backtracked, crossed itself and went at right angles until the trailers were unsure of which tracks they had followed before.

The sheriff sent three men to circle the area, and at last they came up with a new trail. Then almost as quickly they lost it again as it went into the main fork of Broken River. The sheriff sent half his posse on each side of the stream. Jackson could walk his mount up the hock-deep stream for miles if he wanted to.

Dave was on the west side of the river and had ridden half a mile when his paint stumbled and fell. Dave jerked his right foot out of the stirrup and rolled away from the floundering horse. He was unhurt but the paint didn't get up. A whimper came from the horse and Dave saw that its right front leg had snapped. Two other riders came up and they both nodded as Dave drew his Colt and ended the misery of the animal.

Dave got his saddle off the horse and hoisted it into the crotch of a maple, then swung up behind one of the riders and they found the sheriff.

"Figure town's the closest spot to get a new horse, so I'm going back, Sheriff. Joe here said he'd ride me double. Get a fresh mount and I'll come back after you." Dave grinned. "I should be able to find the thirty of you."

The sheriff grunted, his gaze never leaving the ground. "He's headed for Sherman Pass, I'll bet. Look for us up that way. Sherman and then a wide circle around the valley and moving out south."

Dave waved and Joe urged his horse back toward town.

Just an hour later the double-weighted horse plodded into Kings Mountain and Dave jumped off at the livery stable. He picked up his gray and put reins on and led her outside. She seemed ready now.

Dave knew he should get back to the posse, but he had a hunch they were headed in the wrong direction. He was afraid that Slade Jackson had doubled back somewhere and the posse had lost his tracks in the confusion. And while he was here in town there were two things he should do. One of them was at the courthouse.

Something about those land record maps still bothered him. Something that was in plain sight he hadn't seen. He didn't bother asking the clerk if he could see the map, simply walked back and pulled down the one on the homesteads.

Dave tried to use his legal training to help him decipher the map. Was there any pattern? Ranchers were scattered with a good three quarters of the area still in open range. Dave looked again at the map, and this time saw that three new homesteads had been penciled onto the map. All were on the river bottom area from the middle fork and south toward town. Three one hundred and sixty acre homesteads.

He looked at them again, noting the dates entered, and each showed that the recording date was yesterday. Dave's legal training took over as he sifted and processed the information. The three sites were not ideal for ranching. They all had water, and grazing land, but none had access to the higher country for summer range. All were boxed in to the east by the Clinton spread and the Vanderzanden ranch which Contway now ran.

Dave called to the clerk who hurried up.

"Yes, Mr. Kemp?"

"Those new homesteads were just filed on yesterday?"

"Right."

"Who filed on them?"

"Well, the clerk isn't in right now . . ."

"It's a matter of public record. You have to show who filed."

They went back to the big ledger and the clerk opened it to the most recent entry. Dave knew none of the names: Clayton Smith, Virgil Johnson and John Rebner.

"You ever see these men before?"

The clerk shook his head. "Said they came in from Texas and want to start some cattle spreads. Seemed to be traveling together. Knew one another at least."

"Thanks," Dave said and went back to look at the map again. This time he moved up closer to it and stared. He had noticed the small line of dots and dashes on the map before, but it held no meaning. He looked at it, and then moved on, but came back to it. The line ran roughly parallel to the main course of Broken River almost like Middle Fork Road did. But the thin line swung to the right up Broken Main

Fork when the road continued up the middle fork and through Sherman Pass to the north.

The map key. There should be a listing of map symbols on the map. Dave found it in the lower left hand corner. Lines and symbols of many types, including the dot and dash line. Beside the symbol was the explanation: "Original Pacific-Atlantic-North Railroad Line Survey, 1853."

"Not again," Dave thought. Every four or five years for as long as he could remember there was a big rags-to-riches boom in town with talk about the railroad bringing in a spur line from the Southern Pacific line. Everyone would be rich. Whoever owned the property the railroad went across would be reimbursed triple its value in land certificates.

But it never happened, and as Dave figured never would until there was a mighty profitable reason to bring a rail line in here. Another dead end. Anybody who had a tip the rail line was coming through wouldn't have to murder and threaten. They could buy the ranchers out and still make a fortune. Dave left the courthouse and walked quickly toward the Golden Girl saloon. It had to be land and cattle, ground and beef, but just who was behind it? Who had the guts and the guns and the money? On the scale this was moving there were a dozen men in town who could finance it. It wasn't a big money operation, at least not yet. But if it kept going it could gobble up the whole valley. And it would be legal.

Just before Dave went into the saloon he saw a lathered team charge onto Main Street and pull up at the sheriff's office. Dave walked down with the gathering crowd. It was Harley Jones, who had the spread just across the ridge from Dave's on the middle fork.

"Raiders!" The word quickly passed back through the crowd. Dave worked forward so he could see Harley who was talking.

". . . and before we knew it there were four of them. All masked, had gunny sacks tied around their horses' hooves. Shot my foreman when he went for his gun. He's hurt bad. Then they burned me out. Burned every building to the ground!"

Dave turned and hurried toward the Golden Girl. Somebody was starting to push, and hard. Right now Elly was his next stop. He rammed through the batwings of the saloon and saw her in the back booth. Dave went over and slid in opposite her.

Elly shifted in the booth and her udder-like breasts flowed out onto the table. Her small face seemed lost in the sea of flesh, and she was frowning.

"Nothing for you, Davee. There is one hombre in town none of our girls will let within arm's distance. But I hear he's on the run already — Slade Jackson. But, he ain't the same. He hates, but his eyes ain't the same."

"You don't think he's the one who murdered Janie?"

"I don't know, Davee. Men kill for all sorts of reasons, and their eyes are probably all different when they do it." She looked up at him. "Did hear three men came into town from Idaho. Least the word is they got Idaho brand horses." Her smile flashed on. "Now, how about buying yourself a beer?"

Dave stood and shook his head. "Later, Elly, I'm still skunk hunting." He walked out the doors and up the street. The first vacant chair he found he sat in, tilted it back against the wall and pulled his hat down over his eyes. Before he went charging off to find that posse, he had some thinking to get done. He worried it again, tried to plot it out, to dissect it with a lawyer's keen insight. He almost chuckled. He wished he had any kind of insight right now.

At last he did what he always had done when hunting. He put himself in the place of the hunted. What would Slade Jackson be doing now? What would Dave Kemp do if he were in Slade Jackson's position?

Run! But where? Run for help! But where? To someone he knew he could count on for help — to the money, to the man who paid the bill on this scheme. Who had the money? The more Dave thought about it, the more the signs pointed to Hank Contway. The man with the money. Could Contway really be behind this whole affair? Was it his cash and his savvy that had turned this end of the country upside down?

Dave pushed his Stetson back and looked at the sun. It was almost dead overhead. He'd have dinner, then ride for Contway's ranch. An hour later Dave had a flour sack filled with supplies for his saddlebags. The gray was rested and the stable man said he hadn't seen Jackson since he left deer hunting two days ago. Dave believed him.

Dave kicked the gray out of town, riding bareback, and caught a few surprised stares from the townspeople. He would angle back to that maple tree out by the main fork, and pick up his saddle. Then he would have to decide whether to try and find the posse — or play his hunch and take a look at Contway's ranch. If Contway was there, Dave would have a few questions for him. If he could find Jackson there, so much the better.

As he jogged along, Dave knew which way he would head. A man like Jackson, with twelve hours to hide his trail, would be impossible to track. Dave was certain of that now. He would pick up his saddle and then move on north and east toward the Contway ranch. By now the posse would be far to the north and to the west.

# Chapter Twelve

The ranch which had belonged to the late Ray Vanderzanden was halfway to the Circle K, and set to the east and north against the base of the foothills about five miles from town. After picking up his saddle, Dave rode east across the prairie until he came to the cover of the pines. He moved through the timber carefully and it was almost an hour before he saw the Contway place ahead. Everything was as Dave remembered it. He tied his horse well back in the brushy part of the timber and moved from tree to tree until he found a good vantage point as near to the buildings as he could get.

Suddenly four shots blasted from below and Dave edged farther behind the twelve-inch pine. He peered out cautiously and saw a man target practicing — it looked like Curley. Two other cowboys were roping mounts in the corral. He saw no one else. Dave settled to wait. He had lots of time, which is something a man on the run didn't have.

Dave waited as the hands below saddled the two horses and got ready to ride. They were headed west, and each had a packroll, but Dave was sure neither was Slade Jackson. Both were too short and stocky. As he watched, another man came out of the ranch house. It was Contway. He said something to Curley, who saddled a horse and rode toward town.

Dave surveyed the whole spread. He could find no other signs of life. The cook, if they had one, must be at work in the kitchen. No other wranglers appeared, no one moved around the bunkhouse and Hank Contway had disappeared back inside.

Kemp moved to his left to the blind side of the house and crept up to it cautiously. He used what concealment there was and then ran the last few open yards to the solid stone wall of the house. He listened, every nerve now tense and expectant. But he heard nothing unusual. He crawled to the right and edged his head up to look into a window. It was a bedroom and no one was there. He ducked under two more windows and reached the front door. It was slightly ajar so he pushed it open quickly and stepped inside. Dave expected Contway would be in the big parlor with the four-foot fireplace.

He drew his forty-four and moved on moccasined feet toward the parlor, but before he got there Hank Contway walked into the kitchen and right into the muzzle of the Colt.

"Afternoon, Hank. Thought I'd drop in for a talk."

"Kemp! How'd you get in here?"

"Outside, Contway." Dave motioned with the gun held in his left hand, and the other man walked slowly toward the door, looking back in surprise.

Dave herded him around to the back of the house and up a little rise where he could see anyone who approached the ranch. Contway didn't have his guns on. His right arm was in a sling. The memory of the beating he had taken from Contway surged up in Dave and he smashed his right fist savagely into Contway's surprised mouth. Contway took a quick step backwards, then sat down holding his jaw.

"Contway, you were with Jackson when he bushwhacked my pa," Dave said.

"No!"

"The Larchmont brothers hung around the livery stable. They go with Jackson to shoot up my crew?"

"Jackson was a loner. Larchmonts are my men. I hired them."

"Why?"

"My riders, somebody I can trust!"

"Why the big land grab?"

"I don't know anything about a land grab, Kemp."

Dave transferred the Colt to his right hand. "Stand up, Contway!" he ordered. Contway did. Dave swung his left hand backhanded catching his doubled knuckles high on Contway's cheekbone and staggering him backwards.

"Don't lie to me, Contway. The Vanderzanden spread, the Clinton place, now Harley Jones and the grab for the Circle K. What's the whole story?"

"Soak your head, Kemp!"

"Those phony homesteads yesterday. They some more of your men?"

Contway glared at him, and at the same time a pistol cracked, whining a bullet past the two men. Contway dropped behind a tree and Dave jumped for another tree. The shot had come from near the corral. Dave looked at the gunman who was on a horse, a big strong black. The rider turned and snapped another shot at them as Dave fired back. Dave saw him clearly. It was Slade Jackson.

"I'll be back for you, Contway," Dave said as he turned and ran for his horse, three hundred yards up the hill. That would give Jackson a head start, but not enough to matter. Dave hadn't planned on this. Jackson must have come directly here last night, rested all day, and now was on his way south, fast. Dave could see Jackson riding hard along the edge of the timber, northward toward the Circle K. At least it would put them on Dave's home ground. Dave mounted and rode away. In the excitement Dave had forgotten about his arm. Now a soft pounding came through, but it wasn't as bad as Dave thought it would be after he had hit Contway with his right hand.

Jackson skirted the timbered slopes and rode north as hard as he could urge the black. Dave kept the trail but knew he was being outdistanced. Dave checked the sun. It was still three hours to sundown and another hour after that to dark. Jackson could keep on moving in the dark, but Dave couldn't track him. Dave thought of using the rifle, but at this distance it would do no good, and would only warn Jackson that he had a long gun. He would track Jackson as far as he could tonight, then pick up the trail in the morning.

The posse should be somewhere in this area. If the men were here, they might head off Jackson. But Dave was afraid the

135

sheriff would have seen the hopelessness of his chase long before now, and headed back toward town.

The black left the shelter of the pines along the east edge of the valley and plunged into the open range for the three-mile run to the opposite ridge. Dave angled across the gap, forded the river and came up on the opposite bank in time to see Jackson head up Deadtree Canyon. This was the best place to cross the ridge into the middle fork valley of Broken River.

It was nearly five minutes of hard riding before Dave came up toward the canyon mouth. It was an ideal spot for an ambush. A rider moving into that heavy shade of the big oak trees would be blinded for four or five seconds — plenty of time for a good gunman to rip off three or four shots from close range.

Dave stopped back two hundred yards from the mouth of the canyon and looked it over. Then as if he had seen something, he slipped off his horse, grabbed the rifle from the boot and slid behind a small boulder. He listened intently, but could hear no sound.

"Might as well come out, Jackson. Your six-gun's no match for my Winchester!"

An answering shot spit dirt a dozen feet

in front of Dave and he ducked behind the rock. He levered three shots into the huge oak inside the shaded space. He waited a few seconds, then carefully aimed two more shots at rocks just behind the oak. He listened again and this time heard the steady pounding of a horse moving up the hard-beaten trail.

Dave ran for his gray and rode toward the canyon. He used a secondary trail, bypassing the open, deeply shaded entrance, and once on the cattle trail, stopped to listen again. The hoofbeats were easy to hear. Dave rode. There was little chance that Jackson would leave the trail. The brush up the sides of the canyon was heavy, almost impassable, and far too thick for silent movement.

At the far side of the ridge, where the ridge trail entered the valley, Dave looked carefully for hoofprints. The trail led north again. The middle fork was smaller than the stream they just left and had carved out a smaller valley, no more than a half mile wide and narrowing rapidly to the Harley Jones ranch that had been burned.

There was no sign of Jackson, so already it became the slow and tough job of following the trail the big black laid down. Dave leaned to his right watching the ground carefully, and the tracking began.

The prints skirted the valley side, swung into the timber as it passed the burned-out ranch, then shot straight for the northernmost tip of grass before the timber closed in. Jackson was moving faster now. The black's hooves were spreading dirt farther behind the prints.

There was no sign of the posse. It must have turned back.

This time Dave entered the timbered area carefully, but it was not as thick or as dark as he had thought it would be and Jackson would have no good spot to hide. The rider did not know this area, Dave decided, as he crashed brush for half a mile, before his quarry found the game trail that followed the headwaters of the middle fork. They climbed steadily. Dave could not see the sun and almost before he realized it, darkness closed around him, and he was through tracking for the day.

He made camp, and built a small smokeless fire from dry pine twigs and heated water from the stream for coffee. His saddlebag was better stocked this time and even contained some crackers and tinned cheese. Jerky was still the main course.

Dave cleaned his six-gun by the flickering light of the tiny fire, then drowned the flames and rolled up in his blanket with his forty-four close at hand. There was no moon. If Jackson were riding tonight, he would be making very slow progress.

Dave slept well, waking only once when he rolled onto his right arm. He woke just as dawn was tinging the eastern sky. He had a quick cup of coffee and some jerky and when he could see the trail, he was moving up the slope. The game trail became more and more indistinct and at one place led into a secondary valley where the tracks headed straight across. Was Jackson headed for Sherman Pass? Maybe Jackson was cutting for the road now, hoping he had lost his trailer.

But where could he go? Even if he hit the road and punished his black, he was riding into nowhere. There was nothing but a hundred miles of high peaks and rock slides and high plateaus ahead of him. If he pushed a hundred and fifty miles north over the raw country he might find the little town of Pendleton. Where was the man going?

It was almost noon when Dave found the type of tracks he was watching for and knelt down in the soft soil near them. The dirt in the bottom of the hoofprint was almost the same color as that around the print. Dave gouged the sand beside the print, and found it wet, darker. It would take about two hours for the sand to dry this much. He was two hours back, but slipping more all the time.

When the sun was overhead the tracks wandered to the west again. Was Jackson still searching for the Sherman Pass road, or did he have other plans? Dave's arm felt much better today — the healing poultices of Doc Bevins were doing their job. He ate jerky again and finished the tin of cheese and crackers.

Gradually the trail led west and then down toward a clutter of gnarled oaks that were twisted from a sudden flash fire years ago. The area before had been almost tree-less, so he looked forward to the glade ahead. There might even be a spring. He looked over the area carefully, but there was no place for a man and a horse to hide. Anyway, it would be a bad spot for an ambush. He rode in and saw no one. He relaxed and reached for his hat.

"Keep both hands right there on your hat brim, Kemp!" It was Slade Jackson, but still Dave couldn't see him. "Slide off your horse and keep both hands well away from that hardware."

Dave dropped to the ground, hands high.

"Easy, now, Kemp. Unbuckle that gunbelt and drop it."

Kemp did, and by then had spotted Jackson behind a twisted oak fifteen feet away.

"Move over on that rock and lay down on your face."

Dave looked at the gun at his feet and knew it was useless. He went to the rock and lay down. The rock had been spewed up millions of years ago. It was the edge of a dropoff to a small gorge ten feet below.

Jackson came from behind the oak and picked up the gunbelt. Then he took the reins of the gray and moved her down the trail a few yards. He looped the gunbelt around the saddle horn, keeping Kemp in his sights all the time.

"Should have done it right the first time, Kemp," Jackson said. He whistled sharply and the black came trotting up the trail from where he had hidden it.

"By damn! It works! Contway said that black would come a-runnin' if you whistled." The bald man swung up on the horse, but kept the Colt on Dave.

"So long, Kemp," Jackson said and raised the forty-five.

# Chapter Thirteen

Dave whistled the same way Jackson had, and the black shied, then started toward the boulder. Jackson was thrown off balance and had to scramble to hold his saddle. The instant the gun wavered, Dave rolled over the edge of the boulder and squirmed to get his feet under himself as he fell. He dropped about eight feet and hit on his feet and knees then rolled twice. He scrambled back under the protective overhang of the rock and into a crevice. Jackson couldn't see him from above.

He heard Jackson yelling. Dave kicked at a large rock and pushed it down the slope. It crashed through some brush then kept on going down the sharp incline toward the valley below. Dave was safe for the moment.

Dave heard the voice just above him on the lip of the boulder.

"Come on up, Kemp!" Jackson demanded.

There was no reply.

"Know you're down there, Kemp." There was a pause. "Hell, don't make no difference. Got his horse, his gun and his rifle and all his food. If that wasn't him went rolling down that gorge, he can't hurt me much, anyway."

A few moments later Kemp heard the horses' hooves striking the rocks as they moved off down-trail. Dave looked in that direction and could see the trail a quarter of a mile below where it wound around a rocky cliff. Then he remembered. This was Deadend Canyon. They first tried to build a wagon road to the upper ranges through here, but it was a box canyon. A narrow horse trail eventually was blasted out of the side of the cliff.

It would be slow moving for a horse to go down the trail now, after this many years. It could be the edge that he needed. He waited until he was sure Jackson had continued down the trail, then he climbed back to the clearing, and sprinted across it and made his way into the tangle of boulders and brush that swept down the graying ridge. He worked his way down slowly, taking his time and being sure not to make any noise. When he reached the point he had seen before from up the trail, he looked at the ground carefully and made sure that the two horses had already passed.

He moved faster then. He had a half

mile to cover and had to beat the horses there, if his plan were to work. He ran low, screened from the trail by the brush and boulders, and made good time. The spot he wanted was where the trail had been hewn out of the face of the cliff, and the overhanging rock had cracked and fallen away years before. It made a perfect unarmed attack position.

Dave pushed two boulders, as large as he could roll, up to the brink of the cliff and watched the back trail. Soon the lone rider and his two horses appeared. At this point the ledge that the trail was on dropped only twenty feet or so to a second shallow ledge, which then fell away three hundred feet to the core of the canyon far below.

Dave remembered his promise to bring Jackson in alive, and he still hoped to. This was his best chance. He noted with a smile that Jackson held the reins of his gray in his hand. They were not tied together. Dave gave no warning, and when the man and horse were in the right spot, Dave pushed the hundred and fifty pound boulder over the rim and sent it bouncing down the cliff directly in front of the horse.

The boulder smashed into the trail ledge three feet in front of the black. The suddenness of the falling boulder startled the black and he reared. Jackson, who had been slouching in the saddle only half watching the trail, spewed from the saddle and fell partway over the edge of the trail. He screamed and clawed at the loose rock and dirt. But his hands found no grip and he slid over the edge and Dave heard him hit on the ledge below. The black minced backwards a moment, then snorted and started down the trail at a slow trot. The gray stood still.

Dave quickly backtracked until he found a place he could drop down to the trail, then moved along it quickly until he found the gray. He quickly buckled on his gunbelt, then lay down on the trail and looked over the edge. Jackson sat on the edge below. He was moaning.

"Jackson!" Dave called.

The man below looked up in surprise. "Kemp! Get me up from here. I'll do anything you say, just get me up from here!"

"You still have your six-gun?"

"Yeah."

"Throw it over the edge into the canyon."

Dave palmed his own gun up and covered Jackson. He fired once in the dirt near Jackson.

Jackson spat, then tossed the gun over the side.

"Jackson, I should let you rot right there with a couple of slugs in your hide. But the sheriff wants you to stand trial. So I'll drop my rope and you fix yourself a sling around your chest."

Dave found the spot he needed. The trail made a slight bend, and the gray could pull straight back the trail without the rope sliding along the ledge. It might work. Dave dropped the rope for Jackson who tied the sling. Then Dave urged the gray forward four or five steps. But the rope was too short. He took another piece of rope from his bedroom lashing and tied them together. Now the end of the rope would reach the saddle horn. Dave gouged a "V" in the side of the trail to help hold the line.

"Stand up, Jackson. Let's test the sling."

He did and Dave urged the gray to back up half a step. When Dave checked over the side, Jackson was six inches off the ground. Dave went with the gray, urging her, a step at a time, back up the trail. The notch gave way once and the rope slipped a few feet, then caught on a rock and held. The gray backed up again and the rope was firm.

Dave looked over the ledge and saw Jackson turning slowly on the rope, three feet below the ledge. He was unconscious! Dave edged the gray back three more steps, then returned to the ledge and grabbed Jackson's arm. He pulled the face toward him and slapped it several times. Dave knew he would never get the unconscious man off the ledge by himself. He needed Jackson's help.

Gradually Jackson's eyes blinked, then stared in glazed fear at the void below him.

"Don't look down!" Dave commanded. "If you want up here you'll have to help. Can you swing your legs up on the ledge?"

Jackson tried twice and on the third time his boot caught hold of the ledge and Dave grabbed the boot.

"Now try to get the other foot up! Try!"

It took five chances this time before both boots were latched to the ledge. Dave pulled the arms and the rope and kept yelling at Jackson to try to boost himself over. Then Dave looked at the horse. If he ordered her back, and she slackened the rope instead, both of them would go over the edge.

For the first time Dave reached over the ledge with his right hand and grabbed the rope at Jackson's chest.

"Jackson, when I say three we're going to drag you over the edge! This is it. You live or die right here! One, two, three!" Both men strained and sweated and Dave felt his right arm would be torn from its socket. He looked at the horse. It was the only way.

"Back, girl! Back!" he yelled at the mare, and gradually she edged back up the trail and the long slender form of Slade Jackson rolled up onto the ledge.

They both lay there breathing hard, getting some of the strength back that had been drained.

Dave stood first and checked his six-gun. It was dusty but in working order. He untied the rope from Jackson and relashed his gear. He mounted and moved toward Jackson.

"On your feet, Jackson, and walk. The ledge continues for another quarter of a mile. Get up." Jackson sat still.

Dave shot into the rock beside Jackson who heaved up quickly, shied toward the drop-off and then hugged the cliff side and walked forward.

It took them almost a half hour to cover that four hundred and forty yards. At one place the trail had almost been wiped out by a landslide and only three feet of trail remained. In front of it they found the black, head down, waiting. Jackson crawled on his hands and knees across the six-foot section. Dave walked it easily, but the horses had problems. Their flanks rubbed the side of the wall, and they balked. At last Dave tied the reins to his lasso and played it out as he walked across the ledge. Then he stood well back and whistled for the horse and jerked the reins. The black scrambled forward, plunging and smashing into the wall, all four feet ripping and tearing at the scant footing. The black was almost over when his outside hind foot slipped and he fell against the wall, but pawed and scratched and kicked over the last two feet to safety. The gray was smaller and came across with less trouble.

Dave prodded Jackson ahead of him and soon they were off the ledge and back on a solid trail. They moved off the trail and under a clump of oak trees and Dave called a halt. He cut two feet off his lariat and tied Jackson's hands together with a foot of rope between them.

Jackson had recovered from his paralyzing fear of the chasm. "You think this twine is going to hold me from going anywhere?" he asked. "We'll never get to your place before dark. Lots of things can happen before dark, before we get to Kings Mountain."

Dave snorted. "They sure can, Slade. You can wind up dead."

# CHAPTER FOURTEEN

Dave looked at the sky. There was still an hour of light. He knew Jackson was right. A lot could happen before he got his prisoner back to town. Would it be better to stop now and make a good camp, or to ride until he had Jackson in jail? Make camp, Dave decided. Have a good sleep and then he could watch Slade tomorrow and get him into town. Then he had planned on a little man-to-man talk with Jackson. Tomorrow would be better for that, too.

Ten minutes later they were moving down-trail again. Jackson was in front on the black and Dave rode close behind him. Two miles farther down the trail they came into the edge of the valley, where a small stream wound toward the Lewis River. Dave found a spot where the creek swung wide under a spread of young pine and vine maple. He picketed the horses and then had Jackson gather some small rocks for a fire ring.

Fifteen minutes later he had coffee boiling and split the last of the jerky with

Jackson. They made coffee three times in the battered tin can.

Jackson looked at Dave. "You really expect to get me back to town, Kemp?"

"Aim to."

"That could take some doing."

"I know." Dave stood and got the rope from his saddle and tied Jackson's feet the same way his hands were, with about six inches of slack rope between his heels. He put two knots around the slack rope and played out six feet of the lariat which he tied firmly around the trunk of an eight-inch pine a foot off the ground. Dave cut off the ten-foot leftover.

"Hey, what you doin'?" Jackson asked as he watched Kemp's maneuvers.

"Doin'? I'm doin' some of the 'doin' you said it would take to get you into town — alive!"

Dave jerked Jackson's hands over his head and checked the knots. One of them had been half bitten open, so Dave retied it. When it was firm again he tied the end of the lariat around the slack between Jackson's hands, and went to the end of the rope.

"Lay down, Jackson," Kemp said.

"Try and make me!"

Dave wrapped the rope around his hand and lunged backwards. The rope pulled tight and snapped Jackson's arms over his head and his shoulders down onto the ground with a thud. Dave pulled the loose end of rope around another pine and pulled it tight. He tested it. If it were too tight Jackson could strangle on his own unexhaled breath. Dave didn't want that. He wanted Jackson alive and in jail. Dave tied the rope firmly around the tree, then went to where Jackson lay on his back.

"Now, Jackson, I want some answers."

"I don't know nothing."

Dave squatted beside Jackson and back-handed him a stinging blow.

"It figures, Kemp — hitting a man when he's tied down."

"You're not a man, Jackson, you're an animal." Dave stared at the man on the ground. Dave's face was hard, his eyes unblinking. Jackson looked away.

"Who hired you to gun down my pa?"

"President Grant."

Dave backhanded him again. His fist was clenched and Jackson's head rocked to one side.

"Did the Larchmont boys go with you when you killed my crew?"

Jackson stared straight up at the darkening sky.

"Did you kill my sister, Janie?"

The man remained silent.

"Have you been working with Contway on this whole land grab?"

Only silence. Dave reached toward the fire as he talked and picked up a pine branch about an inch thick. One end was blazing. "Jackson, there are lots of ways to make a man talk." Dave held his sheath knife and the now glowing end of the pine branch close to Jackson's face. "Which one should I use, Jackson?"

Jackson rolled partway on his side and faced away from Dave.

"Neither one, Kemp. You ain't got the guts!"

Dave dropped the glowing end of the branch on Jackson's side and watched in fascination as there was a puff of smoke, then a scream from Jackson. Dave jerked the branch up.

"Jackson, did you kill my pa?"

"Yes!" Jackson said in a pain-strangled voice. "Just keep that thing away from me!"

"Did you kill my sister, too?"

"No! My deal was business, just your pa."

"Who paid you?"

"Can't say. He'd kill me!"

"I'll kill you if you don't!" But even as he said it, Dave knew he couldn't. He couldn't stoop to the tactics his enemies were using. He couldn't even use the burning stick again. But he had a confession.

"Tomorrow, Jackson. Tomorrow you'll talk. And don't bother trying to get away. An Indian taught me this rope trick. Nobody's ever got out of it yet."

Dave put some more sticks on the fire, checked his six-gun and his cartridge belt. Then he leaned against a tree and used his blanket as a mattress. It would be a good night to sleep. Cool enough, but not too cold. All he had to do was figure how to stay awake until he was certain Jackson was sleeping. Dave got up and checked his small camp. He rubbed down the gray and checked the pickets of both horses, then changed his mind and moved them to some fresh grass.

Dave sat down and watched the small fire. Jackson looked like he was asleep, but Dave couldn't be sure. He stared into the fire and watched a stick slowly disintegrate and change itself into heat, smoke and ash. It was a slow, monotonous, sleepy sequence. So slow!

Dave jerked his head up and blinked. He had been asleep. How long? He reached for his forty-four. It was still there. He put a few more sticks on the fire and it blazed up so he could see Jackson was still straddle-tied. He hadn't rolled over. Dave looked through the trees at the blue-white stars. He hadn't been asleep long, because Orion's belt was still beaming down through the opening. By morning it would be gone.

He stretched and made a new batch of coffee in the can and sipped it. He had one key to the tragedy that had hit the Circle K, but he had a strong feeling it was only one. There could be two or three keys before he had all the truth unlocked.

When the stars had moved enough so Dave knew it was midnight, he checked his prisoner again, then took the blanket and made his way carefully down the stream two hundred yards, moved back into the brush and quietly spread the blanket. He knew Slade Jackson was beaten for the moment. He would still be there when Dave went back the next morning. Dave went to sleep almost immediately.

When he awoke, he was aware that dawn was at least an hour old. He washed the sleep out of his eyes at the stream and jammed his Stetson on his head as he took the blanket back to camp.

Slade Jackson was still there all right, and yelling to be untied.

"Shut up, Jackson, or I'll put a gag on

you." Dave untied the rope that held Jackson's hands and the man sat up with relief, then stood.

Dave stirred the fire into life and made one more cup of coffee. It was the last of the meager provisions. They would get back to town today or go hungry.

Ten minutes later they were moving down the trail. Jackson was riding ahead. Dave knew the country here. They had entered a small valley that should lead into the Lewis River fork about a mile on downstream. The burned-out Jones place should be just over the ridge to the left and the Circle K about five miles on the left. There was another ranch downstream on the middle fork where they could stop in for some food.

But first he had some work to do with Jackson where there were no witnesses. Dave flexed his right arm and felt only a light sting high in the bicep muscle. He pounded the fist into his open palm and smiled.

They had traveled almost three miles down the valley and had hit the Lewis River and went downstream when Dave stopped. He had left the rope manacles on his prisoner when they started. But it was time he had another session with Jackson.

There was a broad curve in the river here and a grassy, open spot. He dismounted and motioned Jackson down.

"About time, Kemp," Jackson said. "This black's got a stone in his foot."

Dave moved over to the front foot Jackson pointed to. He had just leaned over to lift the hoof when the man hit him. Jackson must have clasped both hands together and swung, because Dave tumbled on his back. He rolled sideways just as Jackson's boots came down in the spot where Dave had been.

Dave was on his feet quickly, shaking his head to clear it, and trying to stay out of the way of Jackson. As Dave's head cleared he saw that Jackson had his hands apart now. He had worked loose the knots on one side and the rope trailed from one wrist.

Jackson came at him in a rush and Dave couldn't escape the flailing arms. They went down in a tangle of arms and legs and Dave rolled free. He felt for his gun, but it was gone. Jackson drove in and Dave hammered him in the stomach, doubling him over.

Dave came toward him slowly and Jackson sprang up, exploding a wicked, chopping fist on Dave's jaw. For a slight man, Jackson could certainly fight.

Then Dave moved in, blocking the fast right hand of Jackson and battering the taller man around his nose and chin with straight left jabs.

Jackson must have sensed he would be outboxed and made a scramble for a pile of rocks. Dave dragged him down from behind, twisted Jackson's left arm behind him and rammed his face into the grass.

They both were breathing heavily. Dave hardly noticed the wound in his arm now. He brought the killer's arm up higher and higher until Jackson yelled.

"Ever had a broken arm, this way, Jackson?"

Jackson heaved up in desperation and unseated Dave who rolled to his right and came to his feet just as Jackson's boot grazed his side. Jackson was coming in again, this time with a rock held over his head. Dave rolled and dodged and the rock crashed onto empty ground. Then Jackson was on top of him, pounding him with fists and cursing him with every blow.

Dave grabbed one of the fists with both hands, pulled Jackson toward him and threw him off the opposite side. He gained his feet before the other man did and was ready for Jackson's charge. Dave waited until the last moment, then dodged to one side and tripped Jackson, who spun past him, and crashed through some brush.

Dave looked for Jackson, who had fallen through the small trees and into a now dry high water channel of the Lewis River. It was only three feet to the bottom of the dry bed, but Jackson had hit his head against a rock. He leaped down the bank to check the pulse in the head of the man. Jackson was still alive. Dave found his hat and dumped a hatful of water in the outlaw's face. Jackson came back to consciousness slowly.

"Had enough, Jackson?" Kemp asked as Jackson began to stir.

The thin man shook his head and hit Dave in the face with a soft punch. Dave let the tall man stand up, then cut him down with two punches. Dave pulled him halfway to his feet. "Did you kill my sister, Janie?"

"No."

Dave hit him again and felt the nose smash when knuckles dug into the gristle as the man flopped to the ground.

Dave lifted him once more. "How are you tied in with Contway?"

"Knew he was in it, somehow. Never told me how."

The uppercut Dave threw caught the

man's chin flush, snapped his head back and pitched him to the ground. Dave brought another hat of water and dumped it on Jackson. Desperate eyes came into focus after a few seconds. Hands went up in front of the outlaw's face.

"Don't hit me again. Don't hit me!" Jackson pleaded.

"Did you kill my sister?"

"No."

"Who killed her?"

"Don't know."

"Who paid you to kill Pa?"

The eyes rolled and then steadied. "Arch Sanco. My pa knew him back East. He paid me."

"Sanco?" Dave spelled it and the bald head nodded. "You knew him by that name back East. What's his name out here?"

"Water," Jackson said. "Drink!"

Dave looked at his canteen on the gray. It was easier to drink from than a hat. He left Jackson and hurried to the horse for the container. When he turned Jackson was crawling toward the top of the river bank, and Dave spotted the lost six-gun laying there. Dave ran back and caught Jackson just as the man's hand closed over the Colt.

Jackson fired before he was ready and the slug missed Dave. Then Dave was on him grabbing the revolver and twisting the handle back toward Jackson. Dave realized he hadn't caught the cylinder and the gun could fire. The roar of the six-gun was almost in Dave's face. Jackson stopped struggling and fell to the ground.

Dave took the gun and saw the powder burns on Jackson's chest and the growing red stain. He stared at the dying man for a moment and saw Jackson try to talk.

"Sanco to meet me tomorrow night, old Indian burial grounds," he said, then lifted his head off the ground and dropped it back as a soft hush of air rushed past his lips.

Dave sat there on his knees looking at the dead man. Here was the man who had killed his pa. He was dead. But vengeance wasn't sweet. It wasn't what he thought it would be. And the killing wasn't through yet.

He tied the body over the saddle of the black. The horse skittered and shied away from the body, but at last settled down to its load.

Dave rode for the Circle K. He couldn't go barging into town with Slade Jackson draped over his horse. Someone in town had to believe that Jackson was still alive so he could meet him the next night at the Indian burial grounds.

It took almost two hours of crossing ridges and rivers until Dave saw the Circle K. He had made a wide track around a group of horsemen, and detoured around one ranch. He wanted to follow up on the plan and go to the meeting in Slade Jackson's place.

Dave cut loose Jackson's body in the willow thicket below the barn, and turned the relieved black into his corral. The horse had Contway's brand on it.

Dave checked the house and buildings and decided the crew was in the hills running down strays. He changed clothes and had some stale bread and preserves, then rode for town.

# CHAPTER FIFTEEN

When Dave rode into Kings Mountain he tied up at the sheriff's office. A new deputy said that the sheriff was eating, and that the posse came back in the morning without Jackson.

Dave spotted the sheriff hunched over a last cup of coffee in the Beefsteak House. As Dave walked in, the sheriff looked up, his eyes tired.

"Where you been?" the sheriff asked.

"Riding. I checked out Contway's place before I caught up with the posse. Flushed out Jackson." Dave looked around the eatery. "Could we talk more in private?"

The sheriff dropped some coins on the table and pushed back his chair. He went out the door without saying a word and Dave followed. When they were in the office the sheriff told the deputy to check out the saloons. When he had left, Sheriff Zedicher nodded.

"So where is Jackson?"

Dave told him about the chase and how Jackson died. "And he admitted he killed my pa," Kemp added.

The sheriff made a small X beside Jackson's name in a ledger he took from his desk. "That's one accounted for," he said as he made the mark. "Now what about this Arch Sanco? No evidence about who he might be?"

Dave shook his head. "But I plan on keeping Jackson's meeting with him." Dave stood up. "I'll check back tomorrow, Sheriff. Want Doc to look at this shoulder again."

Kemp rode to the doctor's office. There were three women waiting, but Dave tipped his hat and scurried past them into the back room. Doc was changing a dressing on a boy's slashed arm. He nodded at the room where Old Charley was.

"Somebody back there wants to see you, Dave. Go on in."

Dave went through the door and stopped. Old Charley was sitting up in bed playing solitaire!

"Charley, you old sidewinder!" Dave said as he walked forward. He extended his hand and Charley gripped it hard. The old wrangler looked at Dave and a low gurgling sound, almost a whimper, seeped from his lips. Tears began rolling down the old puncher's cheeks. He wiped them away and looked embarrassed.

Doc Bevins came through the door. "Charley, don't let this whippersnapper upset you," Bevins said. "He just ain't worth it. Besides, I'll tell him you cheat at solitaire!"

Dave looked at Doc and grinned. "Can Charley help us any?"

Doc patted Charley's shoulder and took a black five off a black four. "We've worked out a type of communication," he explained. "I ask Charley a question, and he answers yes or no. Takes time, but we get there. So far we've put this together." Doc handed Dave a sheet of paper with five numbered points.

1. There were three attackers. He heard them all, but saw only one.
2. The man he saw was not Slade Jackson.
3. One of the men was called "Curley."
4. He heard no noise from the house.
5. He owes his life to Dave Kemp.

Dave folded the paper and put it in his jacket pocket. Then he told Doc Bevins what had happened the last two days.

"Arch Sanco?" Doc said, shaking his head. "Doesn't strike home with me at all.

Sanco is an unusual name. Don't recall any like that here in the last twenty years or so."

"He's here somewhere, because tomorrow night he's got a meeting to make."

"A land grab," Doc said. "Why? Dave, it just don't seem right. Why would somebody want to buy up land when there's plenty left out there to homestead? Sure it's a tough life, and you can only file on a hundred and sixty acres . . ." He stopped. "Guess it would be faster to shoot up a few people and scare some others off . . ."

"So our big problem is who," Dave continued. "Doc, I'd guess there are ten or fifteen men in town who have enough money. The three saloon keepers for a start."

"But you can't walk up to everybody on the list and ask if they used to be called Arch Sanco," Doc said.

Dave lifted the forty-four from his holster and checked the loads. He spun the cylinder and watched the motion. "Charley, we got the man who killed Pa. Did you hear that?"

Charley nodded.

"Now we'll get the rest of them. I don't think Jackson was at the ranch that night. But if you say Curley was, I know who that is!"

Dave looked at the Doc who motioned

him outside. "Charley, you take it easy and get well," Dave said before he left. "Have you back at the ranch in no time." Charley smiled and the trace of a tear seeped out from one eye.

Outside the room, Dave looked at his medical friend. "You had an idea?" he asked.

"Don't think you've got an eyewitness to a killing. Old Charley can't testify," the doctor said.

Dave thumbed his hat back. "You're right, Doc. So I have to try to bluff Curley. I've got to make him show his hand, or break or run."

Dave moved to the side door. "I'll check it out with the sheriff first, in case some lead starts flying."

The old doctor frowned as Dave left. At the sheriff's office later, Zedicher shook his head.

"You said yourself you had a gun on him last time you were there. Think Contway's gonna let you ride in and question his man?"

"Didn't plan on just riding in."

"What did you plan?"

"Not sure. Play it the way it comes. Somehow I've got to scare Curley into thinking I have an eyewitness who saw him shoot up my crew."

Sheriff Zedicher took a long drink from the coffee cup. "How long you been a lawman, Kemp?" he asked.

"I'll make the laws, Sheriff, not enforce them."

"Let me suggest this," Zedicher said. "You and I go over to the Golden Girl and talk with some of the boys about the trouble. When we get a good audience I let slip how we found an eyewitness. Grubline rider coming over the hill when the shooting started. How he saw all three hombres, and thought it was time he came in and identified them."

Dave sat down to listen.

"Then we put my deputy out on North Fork Road," the sheriff continued, "and see if anybody gets word to Curley or to Contway with the news."

"Sounds good," Dave said.

"Let's try it. Now, you got any ideas about this raid on the Jones place?"

"It's all part of the same land grab," Dave said. "They worked the ranches on the Broken River main branch side, now they're moving over to the middle fork." Dave grabbed his hat and settled it on his head with precision. "You thirsty, Sheriff? I had a long ride and need to drown some dust!"

Just after dark, Sheriff Zedicher sent his deputy on his lonely ride, then he and Dave headed for the Golden Girl. They entered the saloon separately. Before he went in, Dave saw the three Box Z branded horses at the tie rail. Box Z was a big Idaho spread. If the riders were part of the whole package, the plan just might work.

It was over an hour later when Dave came up to the sheriff. Dave was staggering just a little. The sheriff was standing at the bar worrying a beer he had made last half an hour. Dave tapped him on the shoulder from behind. The sheriff turned quickly and Dave took a step back uncertainly and his arm tipped over a full mug of beer on the bar.

"Yeah, Kemp. What do you want?" There was a touch of a growl in the sheriff's voice.

"Zedicher, you're a lousy sheriff." Dave's words were slurred just enough to blame John Barleycorn, but distinct enough to be heard.

The bar chatter died out and half the room was watching Kemp.

"What was that, cowboy?"

"You're in here drinkin' 'stead of out rounding up those sidewinders who shot up my whole crew and killed my sister."

169

Dave's voice rose at the end, and cowboys began moving away from the two.

"Kemp, if you was sober I'd tear you apart! You know we're workin' on it. This ain't the place to talk!"

"They killed Janie, and nobody will find them."

"Shut up, Kemp! Keep quiet or I'll throw you in jail as a drunk!"

"Poor little Janie! Some rotten woman killer loose. How'd you like him to kill your daughter? Sheriff supposed to find him. Right?"

The sheriff looked around at the questioning and angry faces and changed his tactic. He talked much more quietly to Kemp, but still loud enough so that the assembled crowd of men, three or four deep, could hear.

"Look, Kemp, be reasonable. We've been working night and day. I rode all night last night. Now just simmer down. I got a deputy to help. And today we had a grub-line rider come in who said he saw the whole thing out at the Circle K. Says he saw all three of the killers and can point them out. Should have them all tomorrow. So just cool down."

Dave weaved a little and caught the bar. "Well, I dunno." He looked around.

"What'd y'a think, cowboy? He doing his job?"

The cowboy who was addressed shrugged and muttered, "Guess so."

Dave looked around, and could hear the word about the eyewitness spreading through the crowd like a dynamite fuse. He threw up his hands. "Well . . . I guess," he said in pretended agreement. "But it better be soon. Hey, barkeep! Where'd my beer go. Somebody spilled my beer!"

A cowhand laughed and it was over. Dave had the beer and drank it slowly, and ten minutes later he stumbled out the batwings and into the street. He moved toward the hotel. It was a long trip, but once inside Dave made a remarkable recovery, slipped out the back door and ran to the alley. He trotted the block to the next street and went up beside the bank building and around to the sheriff's office.

Dave went inside quickly and the sheriff motioned him into the back room where they closed the door. Three cells lined the back of the room.

"You ever give up law work," Dave joked, "you can sign on with a medicine man show, Sheriff!"

"Hope they took the bait. Didn't see Curley there, but those three riders with

Idaho brands were there. If you think they are part of the same grab, we should know something soon. They rode out just after you left."

The door opened and Sheriff Zedicher looked up. He nodded and the deputy came back.

"Three riders, Sheriff," the deputy said. "Pushing hard. They cut along North Fork Road and turned in at the Contway ranch lane. Riding like they had fire on their tails!"

"It could mean anything," the sheriff said.

"And it could mean somebody is ready to run — fast!" Dave countered.

"They'd head south or west out of here, which means they'd have to come back this way," the sheriff said.

"But not necessarily through town," Dave added. "If I was running I'd go around town, pick up the road on the other side."

The sheriff agreed with a nod. "All right, we'll go out toward the Contway place and sit and watch and see if anything happens."

"Something will happen. It's closing in around them."

"If it does," the sheriff said, "we stop them and bring them in for questioning. That's all. No gunplay, unless they shoot first. Joe, you'd better stay here and take care of the tax-paying citizens."

Before they left Dave traded horses with the deputy. His gray needed a rest. Joe would get her into the livery.

The two riders moving out North Fork Road attracted no attention, and soon they were well beyond town. It was as still and clear as Dave had seen it. A quarter moon rode high over silvery wisps of clouds.

They walked the horses, and stopped frequently to listen for hoofbeats. At the lane into the Contway spread they stopped and the sheriff checked his Waterbury. It was just nine o'clock. They waited, talking in low tones that wouldn't travel. But they were downwind from the ranch, which meant they should be able to hear riders coming long before they arrived. Dave hated the waiting. He wished they could ride in and get it over with. But this was the sheriff's show.

At least they were in the right spot. Anyone leaving in a hurry would come down the lane as the safest nighttime track into town. Going around the town would be slower so a rider would want to make time here.

The sheriff had just checked his pocket watch again at nine-thirty when he held up his hand. Dave heard it, too, the steady drum of horses' hooves. How many he couldn't tell. The two men hustled their horses off the road one hundred feet to the side, then came back and squatted in the shallow ditch on each side of the lane. As the sounds drew closer Dave knew it was only one horse, and traveling fast — too fast for a casual ride into the saloon.

When the rider was twenty yards away, the sheriff jumped out into the middle of the lane and lifted his six-gun. He fired once into the air. "Slow down. I'm Sheriff Zedicher!" he called.

The rider changed his direction and rode directly at the lawman. Dave saw the rider draw his gun, but before he could fire, the sheriff had blasted him out of the saddle with two quick shots.

The rider fell to his right, but the right foot caught in the stirrup and the horse dragged him another thirty yards before it stopped, snorting and stamping. Dave came up in front of the animal to calm it and the sheriff dislodged the boot from the stirrup and rolled the body over. A sulphur match flared and Dave knelt down. There was a moan and both men leaned closer. It was Curley Larchmont.

"I . . . I . . . killed Yancy at Kemp's.

Didn't touch the girl."

"Who else was there, Larchmont? Who else?" Dave asked.

The sheriff touched the man's temple and shook his head. "He can't hear you any more, Dave."

They both looked at the body, then Dave went and brought back the horse. Together they draped Curley over his saddle and tied him on.

"Now, Dave, we ride in and see Hank Contway."

It was a quiet ride. There was a good chance those at the ranch had heard the gunfire less than a mile away. There could be a reception. Dave heard the sheriff reloading his six-gun, blowing it out, making sure the cylinder spun freely. Then he eased it back into its leather home.

Dave was still trying to fit this last puzzle piece into place. Jackson killed his pa. Claimed he didn't kill his sister or the crew. Now Curley admitted that he shot Yancy at the Circle K. But who was with him? If Curley went, he'd be tagging after his older brother, Bill Larchmont. And Bill was dead. There was one more. Could it have been Hank Contway? Why not? He brought in his private guns. He'd certainly go along with them.

A lamp burned in the yard near the ranch house, and two windows were lighted. It didn't look like they expected trouble.

Dave and the sheriff stopped outside the rim of light, and the sheriff called out, "Contway! Hank Contway! Sheriff Zedicher. Want to talk."

A figure stepped out on the porch. It wasn't Contway.

"Come on in, Sheriff," the man said.

As Kemp and the sheriff rode in, two other men came to the porch. All wore guns. They looked curiously at the horse with the body on it.

"Contway here?" Sheriff Zedicher asked.

"No, Sheriff," the tallest of the three said. "He had to go into town this afternoon."

"We've got one of your hands here who needs a burying — Curley Larchmont. He drew on me so I shot him."

"Sure, Sheriff. You don't need to explain to us."

"He's all yours. And you'd better unpack those saddlebags. He was ready for a long trip." The sheriff paused. "You the three new hands from Idaho?"

"Why'd you think that, Sheriff?"

"You were riding Box Z stock."

"Yeah, we come from Idaho. Any law against that?"

"Not unless I get a wanted poster on you. Or unless you've been starting bonfires lately." The sheriff wheeled his horse around. Dave turned his mount, too, and they jogged easily out the trail toward town.

"Sure glad we didn't have any gunplay, Sheriff," Dave said, grinning in the moonlight. "And who would ever believe a deathbed confession?"

Sheriff Zedicher turned. "It just depends on who's telling the story, Kemp," he said.

# CHAPTER SIXTEEN

At the end of the Contway lane, Dave pulled up.

"I better check my own ranch, Sheriff. I'll be in town tomorrow about noon to talk over what we'll do tomorrow night down at the old Indian burial grounds."

The sheriff waved. "See you tomorrow," he said, and the men rode in opposite directions along North Fork Road.

Dave was home a half hour later. He rode into the horse corral and stopped suddenly when a six-gun roared behind him.

"Hold it right there, mister. Who are you and what do you want?" one of his riders called out.

Dave lifted his hands. "Kemp's the name, and I'd like some food and shelter for the night."

"Sorry, Mr. Kemp," the rider said. "Didn't know who you was pounding in here that-a-way. Jim told us to keep an eye out since the Jones place burned."

Dave dropped from the horse. "Glad to

see you on the job. Put this nag away, and ask Jim to come up to the house." Dave headed for the kitchen. Suddenly he was hungry again.

There wasn't much food left in the house, and Dave remembered he was past due to bring out some provisions. He'd also have to get a cook and start thinking about running a ranch. Dave had the lamp lighted and was poking in the pantry for some food when his foreman Jim Sanders came in.

"Evening, Jim. Like to have a two-inch-thick venison steak?"

Jim nodded, and they went together to the well house to get the freshly shot venison. Then they talked over the business of the ranch, and Dave found that the spread was in good condition.

"Got a list of things we need, Mr. Kemp," Jim said. "And I figure we'll need three more hands to get that branding done. Like to get it finished soon as we can."

"After tomorrow night, Jim, I should be able to start running a ranch." Dave settled back and looked at the lean, tanned face of his foreman. "You like working a ranch, Jim? Having some say about what goes on, and doing some of the planning?"

"You bet. Always wanted a spread of my own. Somehow just never got together enough cash to set up."

Dave knew he was thinking too far ahead, going too fast. "Let me leave it this way, Jim. One of these days I may be looking for a manager to run the Circle K for me. When I'm ready, would you be interested?"

"Yes, sir!" the foreman said, a smile covering his face.

"We'll talk about it again tomorrow. Say, Jim, what time is it? I'd like to set that big clock."

"I'm no Waterbury man, Mr. Kemp!"

"Sorry, Jim, guess I was in the East too long." Dave said good night to his foreman and finished the steak and fried potatoes and onions he had fixed. He had forgotten how scornful most cowboys were of watches. Cowboys worked by the sun — started and quit, and slept when they were tired. Pocket watches were for Eastern dudes or town dandies.

Dave looked at the small stack of dirty dishes. He would wash them tomorrow. The stack looked bigger and bigger. Now there was a real reason for getting a woman in the house — to do the cooking and the dishes. He thought of Sue Ann and his smile softened a little. Of course there were other reasons, too.

The next morning a summer thunderstorm washed across the prairie and Dave stewed around the ranch until it blew past about ten o'clock. He saddled the deputy's horse then and headed for town. The crew was at work pulling strays in from the timber, getting ready for the branding. Any cow and calf with a Circle K on it was flushed back into the main valley.

It was slow riding on the wet road, so Dave didn't push. He was in town just before noon when the hot sun had dried the street to a soft black mush. Dave's first stop was at the Archer house.

Mrs. Archer answered the knock. "Dave Kemp! Good, I want to talk to you. Come in, come in."

"Mrs. Archer, my boots are full of mud."

"Land sakes, boy. Just wipe the worst off on the little rug there. I've had mud in my parlor before! Now come in."

Dave had known Mrs. Archer all his life, but he had never seen her so excited, so flustered. She looked at him and started to say something. Then she stopped. She took a big breath and began once more. "David Kemp, you've been courting our niece now for, well land sakes, for just

181

years. And I think it's time we ask you your intentions."

There was a giggle from the kitchen door, and Sue Ann came in laughing quietly, a radiant smile on her face. She wore a high-necked print dress and her long brown hair was plaited in twin braids so that she looked about fifteen.

"Oh, Aunt Helen, I didn't think you ever were going to say it. You fumbled around so long." Sue laughed again, and Dave could tell she was delighted. She came to Dave and kissed him lightly on the cheek.

"Now, Sue Ann, this is serious!" her aunt scolded.

"Aunt Helen, I'm serious, too. I realize that life doesn't go on forever. Both Dave and I came very close to being killed up on that mountain. And I don't want to waste any more time being coy and mysterious and unreachable." She smiled at Dave. "As long as the right person is doing the reaching."

Dave took her hand. "Mrs. Archer, you don't have to worry about my intentions. I intend to try to hold her in line."

There was a pause and Mrs. Archer made no move to leave. Dave stood awkwardly for a moment, then said, "I've got to see the sheriff and Doc Bevins. I should be able to stop by tomorrow."

Sue Ann stood on tiptoe and kissed his cheek. "Hurry back," she said.

The sheriff wasn't in when Dave arrived. The deputy said he was checking on a burned-out wagon about five miles south of town.

"Thanks," Dave said. "I'll leave your horse outside. Much obliged for the borrow."

The deputy waved. He was young, not much over twenty-one, Dave thought. He was learning a hard business. Dave took off his hat and resettled it. "Doggone it, Deputy," Dave said. "I had counted on talking with the sheriff this noon. Say when he'd be back?"

"Nope."

Dave slapped his hand against his leg. "Tell him I'll be there tonight where we talked about." He turned and went outside. The street was almost dry now as the hot sun bore down. Dave went to the Iron Kettle, the other eating house in town for a German dinner. He paid for it with a three dollar gold piece and pocketed the change.

An hour later Dave Kemp had traded horses and saddled the gray. He was riding the open range to the west of town. He crossed the Broken River and wandered south. It was his plan to come up on the old Indian burial grounds from the south.

The area was sacred to the Indians who used to live here, but years ago they had been shunted to the reservation, and only the stories and memories persisted. The grounds themselves covered about three acres and lay where Broken River was joined by a smaller stream. The large "V" of land created had been set aside by the tribes as the burial land. There were several types of trees growing here that were not common to the area, and the story was that a favorite tree of a brave would be brought from its native soil and planted over his grave. The trees had a practical purpose, too. Some fall seasons when the great rains came, the Indian burial grounds would be covered with water. Those graves with trees firmly rooted over them would hold the area intact, and the longer the tree grew, the stronger the framework of roots around the spot became.

The tall trees in the plot were natural lightning rods for the whole area, and hundreds of times the Indian trees were struck by lightning, and many had been split, toppled and gnarled over the years.

Dave came into the grounds from the south by fording the smaller stream. He hid his horse at the far southern tip and scouted the area carefully. The natural growth here and the planted trees made it one of the most densely wooded spots in the valley. The north edge of the grounds held a large open space that some said had been used for a council fire area. Others said that Indians would never hold a council so near the dead. But the open space had been preserved over the years by the Indians. Here, too, was a shallow fording area where wagons, stages and travelers could cross over Broken River easily to move to the west cutoff road without going into town and back southwest again.

This would be the best place to watch for a rider coming from town, Dave decided. He was standing under a large maple tree near the edge of the wooded part when he heard a branch snap behind him. He turned, drawing as he did.

"Drop it, Kemp!" a voice demanded. Dave's iron was barely out of leather as he turned, but he saw no one to challenge. He dropped the Colt into the leaves.

A voice laughed. "You would have been

a dead man, Kemp. Least now I know how fast you really are." Sheriff Zedicher dropped from the leafy maple. "I see you got here in plenty of time."

Dave laughed in relief. "You could scare a guy that way, Sheriff." He picked up his Colt, checked it over and wiped it off, then slipped it back into leather. "I figured that story about a burned-out wagon was a blind. What can I do to help out?"

The sheriff reached down for a new blade of grass and chewed on it as he looked around the area. "I can cover this end from the tree," he said. "You ride up the road about half a mile to that big wash. Get your horse hidden in the trees and wait. When a lone rider comes past, you trail him in here."

Dave squatted beside a small fire ring of rocks and poked at the ashes. "That I can do, Sheriff." He paused. "Suppose those three Idaho hands Contway brought in are mixed up in this? Like he wanted a few more guns in case he had to push his way?"

The sheriff toed a stone back into the circle. "That's what I've been wondering. I'd like to connect them to that burning up at Harley Jones' ranch. If I can't, I'll just run them out of town."

Dave resettled his hat and looked at the sun. It was three hours to dusk, but he should be moving. He wanted to be sure and be in position before Arch Sanco came. He might want to check out the place in the daylight, too.

"Think I better find that spot up the draw and get ready for whoever we flush out," Dave said.

"Right," the sheriff said and Dave moved back through the trees for his horse. He rode along the river until he came to the wash which slanted through a dip in the road and up into some brush on the other side. He moved his horse well up into the brush across the road near a tall pine, then angled along the upper slope of the gully to a small pine and a scattering of young willows that would give him plenty of concealment. Dave cut a few branches and dislodged a few rocks so he could have a comfortable waiting spot. Then he put his head down on his arms and closed his eyes.

Pounding horses' hooves woke him. The sun was down, but it wasn't completely dark. In the dusk, Dave couldn't identify the rider who went past, then stopped and walked the horse back. The rider looked at both sides carefully, then got off his mount and led it into the brush on the river side of the road, a hundred yards from Dave.

Dave turned to look toward the gray near the big pine, and hoped that the scent of the other horse had not been picked up. A snort or a whinny from his mount could cause trouble now.

# CHAPTER SEVENTEEN

Time edged slowly by, and Dave let out his breath. If his gray had not sensed the other horse by now, he probably wouldn't.

Darkness closed in quickly and Dave could only guess where the man below him was lying in wait. Who was he, and who was he waiting for? Dave wondered. As he sat there, Dave decided the one below must be watching for Arch Sanco, too. If he were, it could be either to follow him or to ambush him. The man below carried no shotgun, which would be the best choice for a nighttime bushwhacking. If the man did follow a lone rider moving fast on the road south, Dave would follow him. If the one below tried to kill the lone rider, Dave would try to stop him.

Not more than an hour of darkness had passed when Dave heard hoofbeats coming down the road. The morning storm had left a few scattered clouds for the moon to play tag with, but the cover opened and the moon showed a pair of riders with blanket rolls coming from the south headed for town. Dave relaxed as they rode by, un-challenged by the man below.

Dave felt the dampness of the early night dew settle over him. He wiped his face and found his eyebrows already wet. The brush would be wet and slow going when he went for his horse. He would have to time it right to be able to get to his horse and still trail his friend waiting below him. Again he heard a noise.

His head turned slightly to locate the sound. It came from up the trail toward town. He listened, carefully. Yes, it was one rider, and coming fast. Dave watched below, but could see nothing, nor could he hear any movement.

The pounding hooves came closer and closer, then the shadowy form of horse and rider materialized on the road and galloped past, heading south in the moonless shadows. Almost at once there was movement below as the man untied his horse, mounted and picked his way to the road. Dave was moving to the rear to find his mount. The wetness of the evening covered any sound as he saw the horseman below in motion.

When he felt it was safe, Dave ran down the incline toward the tall pine for the gray. The moon was still clouded over, but he found his horse, mounted and moved through the dry wash bottom, as fast as he dared, to the road. He listened at the road and heard one horse pounding down the road. Dave set out at a gallop, but when he was halfway to the burial grounds, he slowed to a cautious walk. He stopped and heard no sound in front of him on the road. The other riders had stopped. He tied the horse to some brush and ran as quietly as he could along the road.

He was three hundred feet away when he heard loud voices. The arguing increased and Dave rushed forward, not worried now about giving himself away.

Two forms materialized before him in the darkness as he slipped from tree to tree. He had forded the creek and was now twenty feet from the council fire area. Two men faced each other, voices ringing. He couldn't make out the problem, or identify the voices. He edged closer.

"I did my part. I fronted you to buy out those ranches. Now I want my money and I want out." It was the whining voice of Hank Contway.

"No," the other man replied.

"You said I could run any time I wanted. Remember? When you talked me into it, you said I could leave with my pockets lined with gold!"

Dave couldn't recognize the second voice. He wished he had a good pine tar torch he could light and run in on them. Still he waited.

"Where's Slade? He was supposed to be here tonight, wasn't he, Arch? Where's he?" Contway continued in his whining voice.

"He's late, Contway. Never was on time. I told him not to run."

"You talk easy, Arch. The sheriff's got witnesses, one anyway. You heard about that grub-line rider! I got to get away! I don't want to hang!"

"You won't hang, Contway, believe me!"

Dave still couldn't recognize the second voice. It seemed to be coming through a mask or a handkerchief. Dave moved closer then and saw the moon break from behind a cloud. Dave caught the gleam of a six-gun sliding from a holster. He drew his own gun and waited.

"Arch, put the gun away! I told you I won't tell nobody about what happened back East. Sure, Slade told me, said it was insurance for me, but I won't tell!"

"Right again, Contway."

As the revolver started up, there was a flash of a shot from the oak tree behind the two men, and almost at the same time

Dave aimed a shot at the bigger man's legs. Then he holstered his weapon and sprinted for the pair. As he got there one of the men was down, and he slammed into the other one, locking his arms around the man's chest and crashing with him into the ground. Then it was a furious battle for survival as the smaller man gouged and kicked trying to get free in a wild surge of fear. Dave watched his chance and smashed a strong right hand to the man's chin, then another and followed it with a neck-snapping left. Contway slumped on the ground unconscious. Dave reached for the man's gun, but it was gone.

Dave looked for the second man, and almost stumbled over a form on the ground.

"Hold it, Dave," the sheriff said. "I shot this one before he could kill Contway. Got a match? Let's take a look and see who it is." Dave found the sulphur matches and struck one. The flickering light showed the pudgy face of Lyle Archer.

"Archer? Lyle Archer?" Dave asked.

The form moaned and moved and Sheriff Zedicher knelt beside him.

"Get a fire going, Dave. He might not be hit bad."

Dave scurried for some dry wood in the brush along the high water line of the creek. When he got back, Archer was sitting against a stump looking haggard but far from dead.

"Slug caught him in the leg," the sheriff said. "I've got the bleeding stopped. He'll live to stand trial."

Dave dropped the wood, and went over to Archer. "Mr. Archer, why? Why did you hire a man to kill my pa?"

Archer took a deep breath and held up a hand in a fruitless gesture.

"Money, David, money. You never get enough. You have a few hundred, you want a thousand. You have a few thousand, you want fifty, a hundred, then five hundred thousand. There will be a railroad through here, eventually, to bring out the cattle and the timber and maybe some coal or gold or silver. The man who controls this valley will be a multi-millionaire. I tried to grab the land with that Englishman. He was an actor from back East. But it just didn't work. Somehow your pa caught on to what I was doing, so I had to kill him.

"But I didn't have anything to do with killing your sister or your crew. That was Contway's work. When I brought him back here he took a fancy to Janie, and went courting. Finally Janie had him thrown off the ranch, and the hands all laughed at

194

him. He wanted revenge."

The sheriff watched Archer as the flames took hold in the dry wood and flickered light over the man.

"What about Jackson, how did he fit?" Dave asked.

"He had known my family in the East, in Boston. I was in a bank there, and took off one weekend with fifty thousand dollars. That kind of money buys a lot out here, least it did twenty-five years ago. Jackson tracked me down somehow, then he demanded money. So I paid him. When Lloyd Kemp had to go, well Jackson was the best man."

A six-gun barked in the shadows and Lyle Archer doubled over. The sheriff and Dave both drew and fired at the flashes of the other gun as it kept shooting. Three more slugs ripped into Archer's body.

When the sound of the last shot faded, Dave took a blazing stick from the fire and moved toward Contway. They found him on his back, his hand still clasped on the six-gun in a death grip.

Back at the fire, the sheriff took off his hat and wiped the perspiration off his forehead with his sleeve. "It's a good thing Contway was aiming all of his slugs at Archer. He had us cold, all three of us, but he just wanted Archer."

"Archer is dead?"

The sheriff nodded.

Dave sat beside the fire, tossing twigs into it, watching the sticks blaze up and disappear.

The sheriff looked down at Dave. "Forget it, son. Forget all about it. Look, I've seen more than my share of men killed in the past twenty years. I'll never get used to seeing a man's life running out a hole I just rammed into him. But sometimes in this end of the country it has to be done."

He paused and looked at Dave. "At least this all clears up one thing. None of these people were involved in your mother's death ten years ago. Must have been some stranger moving through the country."

Dave nodded. That was settled, too, now. He threw a larger stick into the fire, and watched it blaze up. "What are you going to tell Lyle Archer's family?"

"The truth, I guess."

"This could split Kings Mountain wide open," Dave said.

"A whole blasted town founded on stolen money! This won't make my job any easier."

"Soon as word gets out, we'll have our share of new gamblers and swindlers and gunslicks piling into town," Dave added.

"Maybe we won't," the sheriff said. He tossed a branch into the fire and they both watched it quickly flame up, then turn into ashes and fall away to nothing.

"Don't see how you can stop it, Sheriff."

"Try this. Lyle Archer came out here with us tonight as a deputy. We knew there was to be a meeting between Jackson and whoever was behind the land grab, only we didn't know who it was. We laid a trap and caught Contway. We had him cold. Then on the way back to town he pulled a hidden derringer and shot Lyle before we could riddle Contway."

Dave dropped a leaf on the fire. "What's that going to buy us?" he asked.

"Plenty," the sheriff said. "Right now we got a law-abiding town, good cattle business, a school, even a church and a lot of folks who want to raise their kids here. If we tell everybody the town was founded on stolen money, that our leading citizen was trying to land grab the whole valley and that he had people killed, we'd have all that fast-money trouble riding into town for their share of the dirty gold."

Dave watched a stick dissolve into heat and ash, then he looked up. "Burn it away clean?" He nodded. "It might work. I don't see what it could hurt to try."

The sheriff stood up. "Kemp, we'd better get my dead deputy, Lyle Archer here, and that killer, Contway over there, back into town."

Later that same evening, Sheriff Zedicher and Dave walked up the path to the Archer front door. Dave knocked, but the sheriff stood in front of the door as it opened.

"Mrs. Archer, could we come in, ma'am. We have something to tell you."

Helen Archer had broken down and cried. Then she asked about the details and the sheriff told her that Lyle Archer was a hero. It was almost an hour before they could leave.

Sue Ann walked with them to the gate. The sheriff mounted and rode away as if they weren't there.

Sue leaned into Dave's arms and he held her tightly as she cried. He stroked her hair gently and talked to her. At last she leaned away from him. Her crying had stopped.

"Will you come tomorrow and help me with the funeral arrangements?"

He said he would and then kissed her forehead. He knew they would have many tomorrows together, from now until the end of their lives.

The employees of Thorndike Press hope you have enjoyed this Large Print book. All our Thorndike and Wheeler Large Print titles are designed for easy reading, and all our books are made to last. Other Thorndike Press Large Print books are available at your library, through selected bookstores, or directly from us.

For information about titles, please call:

(800) 223-1244

or visit our Web site at:

www.gale.com/thorndike
www.gale.com/wheeler

To share your comments, please write:

Publisher
Thorndike Press
295 Kennedy Memorial Drive
Waterville, ME   04901